Treasure Island

A Play in Four Acts and Ten Scenes

By Jules Eckert Goodman

Dramatized from the novel
by Robert Louis Stevenson

A SAMUEL FRENCH ACTING EDITION

SAMUEL FRENCH

FOUNDED 1830

New York Hollywood London Toronto

SAMUELFRENCH.COM

TREASURE ISLAND.

CAST.

Jim Hawkins
Mrs. Hawkins
Dr. Livesey
Squire Trelawney
Captain Smollett
Redruth
Hunter
Joyce
Allen
Gray
A Fruit Seller
Bill Bones the " Captain "
Black Dog
Pew
Long John Silver
Cptain Flint......................*The Parrot*
Morgan
Anderson
George Merry
Israel Hands
Dirk
O'Brien
Arrow
Dick
Ben Gunn.......................*The Maroon*

TREASURE ISLAND.

THE SCENES OF THE PLAY.

The story of " Treasure Island " is so well known that only a brief résumé need be indulged in here to freshen everybody's memory, and how can this be done half so well as in the words of the immortal little hero, " Jim " Hawkins:

" Squire Trelawney, Dr. Livesey, and the rest of these gentlemen having asked me to write down the whole particulars about Treasure Island, from the beginning to the end, keeping nothing back but the bearings of the island, and that only because there is still treasure not yet lifted, I take up my pen in the year of grace 17—, and go back to the time when my father kept the 'Admiral Benbow' Inn, and the brown old seaman, with the sabre cut, first took up his lodging under our roof.

"I remember him as if it were yesterday, as he came plodding to the inn door, his sea-chest follow-behind him in a hand-barrow; a tall, strong, heavy, nut-brown man; his tarry pigtail falling over the shoulders of his soiled blue coat; his hands ragged and scarred, with black, broken nails; and the sabre cut across one cheek, a dirty, livid white, I remember him looking round the cove and whistling to himself as he did so, and then breaking out in that old sea-song that he sang so often afterwards:

> 'Fifteen men on the dead man's chest——
> Yo—ho—ho, and a bottle of rum.'"

TREASURE ISLAND.

ACT I.

Scene :—*Interior of " Admiral Benbow Inn "'. Before the curtain goes up there is heard singing in loud boisterous voices. When the curtain rises the* Captain *is seen seated at the head of the table with five or six men about the table. (Stools for table—not chairs) All drinking and the* Captain *browbeating them.*

Captain. (*Seated table* R. *Singing with villagers before curtain goes up*)

" Fifteen dead men on a dead man's chest
Yo—ho—ho, and a bottle of rum.

(*Curtain. Cross to head of table* C. *Sits*) Wait! Wait I say—We'll sing that over and louder—every-one of you sing—Sing now—(*They sing*)

Fifteen dead men on a dead man's chest
Yo—ho—ho, and a bottle of rum——
Drink and the devil had done for the rest——
Yo—ho—ho, and a bottle of rum——

(*Hits on table with his tankard*) That's enough—Silence I say! (*As a man gets up*) Where you going?
Man. I am going home, sir——
Captain. (*Thunders at him*) Sit down! Sit

down!—by thunder you'll do as I say—(*The man fearfully sits down. The* CAPTAIN *draws his cutlass and places it on the table in front of him*) Not one of you leaves, do you hear?

THE MEN. Yes—Yes——

CAPTAIN. It's a foggy evening and I'll have company—company—(*Hits on the table with the end of his cutlass*) Mrs. Hawkins!—Mrs. Hawkins I say——

(MRS. HAWKINS *rushes in from the taproom* L. C.)

MRS. HAWKINS. (L. *of table*) Yes—yes, Captain——

CAPTAIN. Why don't you come when you hear me—More drinks, Mrs. Hawkins——

MRS. HAWKINS. (*Pleadingly*) Oh, please—please, sir——

CAPTAIN. What! Did you hear what I said! Did you!

MRS. HAWKINS. Very well, sir, I'll get it! (*Goes out to taproom* L. C.)

CAPTAIN. You two, there—what were you whispering about—I saw you—I'll have no whisperings, you hear—Well—Why don't you speak?

A MAN. If you please, sir——

CAPTAIN. Who told you to speak—(*Hits on the table with end of cutlass*) Mrs. Hawkins! Mrs. Hawkins!—I'll have the rum! Rum! Rum you hear?

A MAN. Let me go get it for you, sir.

CAPTAIN. Sit down.

ANOTHER MAN. (*Getting up*) It's late and we must go——

CAPTAIN. Sit down, I say! (*The men sit down*) Not a man leaves—I'll not be left alone with those faces out there in the frog——

A MAN. But there are no faces——

CAPTAIN. Who asked you to speak—By thunder,

I've seen men run through for less—Rum! Rum!
Rum!

MRS. HAWKINS. (*Coming in with tankards of
drinks.* R. *of table*) Coming—Coming, sir——

THE MEN. (*Getting up*) But indeed, we've had
enough——

CAPTAIN. What's that——

ANOTHER MAN. (*Getting up*) And we must go
home, sir——

CAPTAIN. What!

(*Enter* DR. LIVESEY.)

MRS. HAWKINS. (*Pleadingly*) Oh, please, sir—
you're driving all my business away———

CAPTAIN. Driving it away—I'm holding it here,
madam. Sit down—(*As the men still stand and
edge toward the door*) What, you refuse—You
refuse to sit down and drink with me—Then, by
thunder, we'll see.

(*With a cry the men rush out* R. C. *The* CAPTAIN
*rushes up to go after them and comes face to
face with* DR. LIVESEY *who enters.*)

DR. LIVESEY. (R. C.) Hello! What's all this!

CAPTAIN. (L. C. *Thunders at him*) Silence between decks!

DR. LIVESEY. Are you addressing me, sir!

CAPTAIN. Aye, that I am! (*Pounding on the
table with the end of his cutlass*) Silence, I said!
Silence—or——

DR. LIVESEY. (*Firmly*) Stop that!

CAPTAIN. What's that?

MRS. HAWKINS. (*Comes down* R. *Terribly
afraid*) Oh, please sir, please——

CAPTAIN. (*Coming up angrily toward* DR.
LIVESEY) Now say that again!

DR. LIVESEY. I said for you to stop it and I
mean it!

CAPTAIN. (*Holding his cutlass in his hand*) Why you rum puncheon—weak-livered swab—you bandy legged lubber—I'll show you!

DR. LIVESEY. (*Firmly*) Put down that cutlass——

CAPTAIN. What you——

DR. LIVESEY. (*Staring* CAPTAIN *down*) Put it down, or upon my honor you shall hang next assizes—Put it down—(DR. *points. The* CAPTAIN *gives way*). And now you listen to me—I warned you against drinking *before*—You had a stroke and much against my will I dragged you headforemost out of the grave—And now, Mr. Bones——

CAPTAIN. That's not my name——

DR. LIVESEY. Well it will serve alright—and I tell you this—one glass of rum won't kill you, but if you take one you'll take another and I'll stake my wig if you don't break off short, you'll die—you understand? Die and go to your own place like the man in the Bible——

CAPTAIN. Well, that's my business——

DR. LIVESEY. Yes, and this is mine—I am a magistrate as well as a doctor—and if I find the least complaint about you hereafter—I'll take means to have you routed out of this—Now then away with you!

CAPTAIN. This is a free inn——

DR. LIVESEY. You heard what I said—Go!

CAPTAIN. (*On stairs*) You'll pay for this—you'll see—(*He starts upstairs*)

DR. LIVESEY. That's alright. And remember the very name of rum is death for you.

CAPTAIN. (*Goes out. Door upstairs*) Huh!

MRS. HAWKINS. (*Very afraid*) Oh, sir, I'm so glad you came—he's got all the people round here so afraid they'll hardly come to the inn any more—we're all in mortal terror of the man, sir!

DR. LIVESEY. In spite of my warning that it would kill him, he's been drinking, eh?

Mrs. Hawkiny. (*Sits*) Oh, yes, sir—drinking and singing that horrid song—and blowing his nose so loud, sir, it sounds like the report of a cannon— (*As* Dr. Livesey *smiles*) You may laugh but I never knew a man to put such fierceness into the blowing of his nose. And when I asks him for money, sir—why—why that's when he blows his nose the loudest.

Dr. Livesey. I dare swear he owes you for his lodgings.

Mrs. Hawkins. That he does, sir. Oh, I appeal to you as magistrate—he's ruining me, sir—ruining me! (*Placing chair* C.)

Dr. Livesey. Mrs. Hawkins—Squire Trelawney and I have been watching your lodger for some time.

Mrs. Hawkins. (*Mysteriously*) He's given Jim a silver penny every month to keep his eye open for a sea-faring man with one leg!

Dr. Livesey. Ah, has he now!

Mrs. Hawkins. And that's the worst of it—the influence he has over my boy——

Dr. Livesey. Jim's a good boy, I'll be bound——

Mrs. Hawkins. That he is, sir. Jim's the best boy in the world. The Captain is filling his head with stories—you should have heard the stories as he told about that boat—(*Indicates picture over mantel*)

Dr. Livesey. (*Looks at picture and reads title*) Flint's Treasure Ship.

Mrs. Hawkins. He's got the boy so worked up, with his horrid tales of pirates and sea fights and treasure hunting that the lad is fair bewitched with the idea of going to sea—and—Oh, sir—(*Rise*) He's all I have. I want my money but I don't want my boy in his company. (*Puts chair back to table*)

Dr. Livesey. I think I can promise you both, Mrs. Hawkins—Squire Trelawney is to meet me here to-night——

Mrs. Hawkins. Oh, sir, I hope there isn't going to be any fighting——

Dr. Livesey. Can you keep a secret, Mrs. Hawkins?

Mrs. Hawkins. As close as the grave, sir——

Dr. Livesey. You can, eh? Come here to the window—(*As she starts to the window*) No, it's so foggy you can't see—but there's a little lugger down at Kitt's Hole—I suspect that's the boat our friend is looking for——

Mrs. Hawkins. What—what is it?

Dr. Livesey. (*Confidentially*) Smuggler——

Mrs. Hawkins. Oh!

Dr. Livesey. That's what your Captain is—that's why he's waiting for one special seaman—and that, Mrs. Hawkins, is what the Squire and I have been waiting for—I've got men all over the countryside—Now, if we can keep an eye on the Captain—(*Enter* Jim *from taproom*) we'll get the whole crew of them—Oh, I say—You say Jim is close to the Captain.

Mrs. Hawkins. Hand and glove—more's the pity.

Dr. Livesey. Jim.

Jim. Yes, sir—Come over here——

Mrs. Hawkins. (*Crossing*) That horrid man has had enough for to-day. The doctor wants to talk to you—(*Exits*)

Dr. Livesey. Sit down.

Jim. (R. *Comes over and sits at the table*) Thank you, sir.

Dr. Livesey. Jim, since your father died your mother has had only you to help her——

Jim. I do my best, sir.

Dr. Livesey. I know you do—quite right, my boy. Jim, your mother tells me the Captain hasn't paid for his board and lodging.

Jim. He hasn't. Not since the first day, sir. He was at that door calling for a glass of rum, " This is a handy little cove," says he. " Much company?"

DR. LIVESEY. Oh, he asked that, did he?

JIM. And when he heard as how there was very little, he says, "This is the berth for me." So in he comes with his sea-chest, and throws down three pieces of gold. " You can tell me when I've worked through that," says he.

DR. LIVESEY. Well, he has " worked through " it, hasn't he?

JIM. Oh, yes, sir, and much beside.

DR. LIVESEY. Jim, if your mother is to get what's owing her—you must watch his every move to-night—I shall be there in the village—the least thing that looks suspicious—any strangers that call him—any attempt of the Captain to leave—you send me word—by your mother—no matter what happens—don't you leave him for one moment——

JIM. (*Slightly afraid but trying to hide it*) Yes, sir—no, sir—yes, sir—(JIM *sits* R. *of table*)

DR. LIVESEY. Jim, there's a nasty fog out there— a fog, that hides things on the sea—A fog like that is bad for ships on good business, but it's good for ships on bad business—These men are on bad business—(*With sudden change of tone*) Hawkins, I am a magistrate——

JIM. Yes, sir——

DR. LIVESEY. Hawkins, I appoint you an officer of the crown——

JIM. (*Startled, arises*) Dr. Livesey.

DR. LIVESEY. (*Salutes him*) An officer of the crown, Hawkins!

JIM. (*Awkwardly returns the salute*) Aye— aye, sir!

DR. LIVESEY. You're the only one who can watch without suspicion—You're not afraid, Hawkins?

JIM. (*Fearfully*) No—no, sir—I—I'm not afraid——

(DR. LIVESEY'S *hands on* JIM'S *shoulders.*)

Dr. Livesey. Then we'll unravel this mystery before midnight—Keep your eyes open—Remember —officer of the crown! (*Exits* Dr. Livesey r. c.)

(Jim *salutes. During the last two preceding speeches there is heard a song as if the singer were approaching.*)

Captain. (*On stairs*) Jim, is he gone?
Jim. Who?
Captain. That swab of a doctor——
Jim. Yes.
Captain. Then go fetch me some rum, Jim——
Jim. But——
Captain. Rum—a whole tankard of it—fetch it to my room. (*Starts away*)
Jim. But, Captain—the doctor said——
Captain. The doctor be blowed—I—(*With sudden change of manner. He now becomes almost whiningly kind*) Nay—come here, Jim—I'm not meaning to be hard with you—you've been my friend—You're the only one I can trust. (*Confidentially*) And if ever I need someone it's to-day —there's things brewing to-day, Jim. (*Looks fearfully over his shoulder at the window*) I can feel it in the air.
Jim. It's just the fog, Captain.
Captain. Aye—the fog. It's full of faces, Jim —the fog—(*Keeps looking around furtively at the window*) Every step of the way from the cove I've seen 'em—faces Jim—like those of Flint's crew up there—They've been all around me—they're—(*Suddenly stares at the window*) See—see there at the window—look——
Jim. (*Crosses to window* c.) Why, there's nothing there!
Captain. Didn't you see a face—a face with an ugly look on't.
Jim. (*Goes to the door* r. c. *and looks out*)

There's not a person on the road.   (*Comes back into the room* c.)

CAPTAIN.   Faces—faces—everywhere in the fog —(*Turns suddenly*) You've kept your eye open for a sea-faring man with one leg?

JIM. Yes, sir—though it's no pay I've had these several weeks. (*Down* c.)

CAPTAIN. What! (*Roars at him*)

JIM. I said I'd had no pay—and—(*As* CAPTAIN *takes out his handkerchief to blow his nose*) That's alright, sir. You needn't mind.

CAPTAIN. (*Blows his nose*) No pay, eh. Well —well—(*Starts to roar and then changes his mind*) Well, there's your pay, lad—take it—take it—I'm needing friends to-day—(*As* JIM *takes the money*) There's a little lugger down at Kitt's Hole—Keep your eyes open—watch the road—and—Jim—any-one asks for me—you don't know me. You never heard o' me? Understand?

JIM. Not even the sea-faring man with one leg?

CAPTAIN. No! None of 'em—Bring my rum upstairs now—and keep your eyes open—(*Turns and glances at window*) There—there he is again— see 'im lookin' in that window.

JIM. I tell you there's no one—nothing.

CAPTAIN. Nothin', eh? It's the whole crew of 'em in the fog there—the whole crew of 'em—and it's going to be a fight—but we'll beat 'em yet— Give me that rum—quick—(*Goes upstairs*)

(JIM *goes timidly to the window and looks out; then he draws back. Finally he gets up his courage and goes to the door, looks out timidly, then grows bolder, goes outside, looks up and down and finally comes in and closes the door. He exits to the taproom. For a moment the stage is empty. Upstairs the* CAPTAIN *can be heard singing his song. Finally a face is seen peering at the window. Then the face disappears and soon the door opens and a man enters. "A pale tallowy creature, wanting two fingers of the left hand, and though he wore a cutlass he did not look much a fighter." He is* BLACK DOG. *For a moment he stands listening to the singing and nodding sardonically. He is making for the entrance upstairs when* JIM *returns with a tankard of rum.* BLACK DOG *wheels quickly at* L.)

JIM. (*Surprised and startled* L. C.) I—I didn't hear you come in——

BLACK DOG. (L. *at stairs*) Umph!—Tidy little place Very tidy. Come here, sonny. Come nearer here. And what have you there? (*Goes up to* JIM *who tries to draw back*)

JIM. Some rum, sir——

BLACK DOG. (*Sniffs it*) Um—rum it is—good, strong rum——

JIM. (*Fearing he is to take it*) It's for the gentleman upstairs, sir.

BLACK DOG. For the gentleman upstairs. Good strong rum for the gentleman upstairs—You know what I think?

JIM. (*Back down* C.) No, sir.

BLACK DOG. I think it is just the sort of stuff that'd suit my old mate, Bill—Now, what do you think?

JIM. I don't know your mate, Bill, and so——

BLACK DOG. Don't you, now—that's too bad—What might you call your—gentleman upstairs?

JIM. Captain.

BLACK DOG. Well, my mate Bill might be called Captain——

JIM. (*Starting to go*) I'm sure he isn't the same——

BLACK DOG. We'll put it for argyment your cap'n has a cut on one cheek—and that the right one—(JIM *starts*) Ah, well—I told you—Now, is my mate, Bill, here?

JIM. (*Up two steps*) I'll go upstairs and let him know——

BLACK DOG. No, you won't. (*As* JIM *still starts to go, he thunders at him*) Stop, I say, or—Stop!

JIM. But, sir, I must tell the Captain.

BLACK DOG. (*Then fawning again as* JIM *stops*) There—there—lad—I'm meaning you no harm. Why, I have a son of my own as like you as two blocks and he's all the pride of my 'art. But the great thing for boys is discipline, sonny. But you see I planned this as a great surprise to Bill—bless his 'art—and I couldn't have you spoil it. (*He takes out his cutlass and tries it*)

JIM. Oh, sir—I hope there's not going to be any trouble——

CAPTAIN. (*Upstairs*) Jim! Jim! Where's my rum!

BLACK DOG. (*Motions* JIM *to keep silent*) Sh-sh! Bill and me's old friends—he'll be glad to see me—Bill will. Bless his 'art——

CAPTAIN. (*Still upstairs*) Jim—Jim——

BLACK DOG. Sh-sh—not a word—or I'll wring your neck. (*Grasps* JIM *by the throat and urges him back of the stairs* L.)

JIM. What are you doing, sir?

BLACK DOG. Giving Bill a surprise—a little surprise.

(*The* CAPTAIN *comes down the stairs.*)

CAPTAIN. (*Furious*) Jim! Where has he gone—Jim, I say—(*Goes to* C. *head of table*) Jim!

BLACK DOG. (*Speaks when* CAPTAIN *gets above table. Steps out with cutlass drawn as* CAPTAIN *turns*) Hello, Bill!

CAPTAIN. (*Stops short as if stunned*) You— you——

BLACK DOG. Come, Bill. You know your old shipmate——

CAPTAIN. Black Dog! What do you want?
(*Moves toward him*)

BLACK DOG. Just come to see my old shipmate,
Billy, and talk over old times.

CAPTAIN. (*Bitterly*) Old times, huh? (*Moves
toward* BLACK DOG)

BLACK DOG. (*Circles to* R. *of table*) A sight of
times we've seen Bill, us two, since I lost them
talons. (*Holds up mutilated hand*)

CAPTAIN. Now, look here, you've runned me
down—here I am. Well then, speak up! What is
it?

BLACK DOG. That's you, Bill—always to the
point. (*Significantly to* JIM) I'll just have a glass
of rum.

JIM. Here, sir. (*Makes as if to offer the
tankard*)

BLACK DOG. (*Sinister*) That's for the gentleman upstairs—I'll have my own—(*As* JIM *hurries
toward taproom*) Don't hurry back. (JIM *takes
hold of the taproom door to close it*) Leave that
open! None of your keyholes for me, sonny.

(JIM *goes out at taproom door.*)

CAPTAIN. (*Fiercely*) Well, out with it——
BLACK DOG. Now, we'll talk square like old ship-
mates.

CAPTAIN. Old shipmates, huh?

BLACK DOG. Sure, Bill—we're all here—Morgan
and Hands and Pew and O'Brien.

CAPTAIN. Silver?

BLACK DOG. Aye, Silver. He's in command
down there on the little lugger——

CAPTAIN. A nice little lugger it must be.

BLACK DOG. We all sailed with Flint and what
we got like gentlemen of fortune belonged to——

CAPTAIN. Flint——

BLACK DOG. Aye, to Flint; and Flint to Flint's

crew—and that's what we've come for—what we're going to get.

CAPTAIN. Go on. Out with it all.

BLACK DOG. There's money about you, Bill Bones—(*Sits* R. *of table*) Money as belongs to us all—and more than money there's a little chart—Flint's fist—showing where all Flint's Treasure is hid—them things belongs to us all and by thunder them things we're goin' to have. Now you know, Bill.

CAPTAIN. And that's the message they sent by you?

BLACK DOG. Aye——

CAPTAIN. Then you can go back and tell 'em I'm still cap'n—and what I say is law—why you mess of swabs—you think you can give your orders to me- –you——

BLACK DOG. It's more than that we'll be giving you—the little Black Spot——

CAPTAIN. Oh, you will, huh? You'll tip me off the Black Spot—well' let's see the one of you that dares—Send him along—or maybe you've got it. Have you? Have you? (*Raises his cutlass and rushes at* BLACK DOG *who avoids him*) Now, hand it over—hand it over——

BLACK DOG. I haven't it—but here it'll be alright—and you'll surrender things as don't belong to you or you'll swing——

CAPTAIN. I'll swing? Then, we'll all swing—and you can tell that to Silver—to Pew—to Hands—to O'Brien—to all of them. Bill Bones is still in command——

BLACK DOG. And that's the answer I'm to take back——

CAPTAIN. Yes. That's the answer and that—that—that. (*As he speaks he strikes with his cutlass.* BLACK DOG *tries to parry and fight, but he is quickly disarmed and flees and the* CAPTAIN *hurls his cutlass at him as he runs out the door. The* CAP-

TAIN *very much shaken himself follows to the door to pick up his cutlass and calls after* BLACK DOG) Tell that, too. Tell them whether Bill Bones has lost his arm—(*As he picks up his cutlass*) Tell that to the one who's to bring the Black Spot and—(*As he comes back into the room he suddenly totters and falls upon a stool*) Jim! Jim! (*The* CAPTAIN *seems about to swoon*)

JIM. What is it, Captain? (*With rum for* BLACK DOG)

CAPTAIN. Rum—rum—quick——

JIM. (*Rum on table* C.) The doctor warned you——

CAPTAIN. Look you, Jim, how my fingers fidget. I can't keep 'em still, not I. If I don't have a drain o' rum, I'll have the horrors; I seen some on 'em already. I seen old Flint in the corner there, behind you; as plain as print, I seen him; and if I get the horrors, I'm a man that has lived rough, and I'll raise Cain. The doctor himself said one glass wouldn't hurt me, and I've hardly had a drop to-day. I'll give you a golden guinea for a noggin, Jim.

JIM. You shouldn't touch the stuff, sir—(*Handing him the tankard*) There. (*As* CAPTAIN *drinks*) Oh, sir, I'd better call someone—I fear it's another stroke.

CAPTAIN. (*Holding on to* JIM) Don't you leave me—don't leave me, Jim—not now—I need you. (*Drinks*) You're the only one worth anything—and with your help—Jim, I'm going to beat 'em, yet—I will, Jim—I will! (*Drinks and seems to recover as he does so*)

JIM. You shouldn't touch that stuff, sir.

CAPTAIN. Eh?

JIM. The doctor said it was sure death.

CAPTAIN. What's he know about it? Doctors is all swabs, and that doctor there, why, what do he know about sea-faring men? (*Rise*) I been in places hot as pitch, and mates dropping round with Yellow Jack and the blessed land a-heaving like the sea with earthquakes—(*Drops glass*)—what do the doctor know of lands like that?—a—and I lived on rum, I tell you. It's been meat and drink, and man and wife, to me, and if I don't get me rum, I'm a battered old hulk on the lee shore. My blood'll be on your head Jim—and on that doctor swab. You will give me one more noggin, won't you? (*Seems to grow fainter*)

JIM. (*Giving it to him from shelf up* C.) You're killing yourself.

CAPTAIN. (*Recovering*) Now, listen, Jim—that man just here—he's a bad 'un—but there's worse put him on—and they're out there on that ship— in the fog—waitin'—they're trying to get me—to tip me the Black Spot.

JIM. The what?

CAPTAIN. The Black Spot—that's about the worst disgrace can come to a pirate Captain—it means he must step down—that he's gone—done for—that he's got to do what his men say instead of them doing what he says—sometimes it means worse than that, too—that's what I'm fearing from that crowd out there—take a look at the door.

JIM. (*Looks out of door*) No one, sir.

CAPTAIN. Close the door. Come here. (*Confidentially, as* JIM *comes up*) It's up there in my old sea-chest—what they're after—but I'm going to try to get away first—and if I do—I'll promise you—I'll come back for you some day—and we'll go to sea—ah!—Aye, as I told you—in a schooner with a piping boatswain and pig-tailed singing seamen—to sea, Jim, bound for an unknown island to seek buried treasure—You'd like that?

JIM. Oh, yes——

CAPTAIN Well, I'll promise you—but if they tip me the Black Spot first you get word to that doctor magistrate—tell him to pipe all hands—and he'll lay 'em aboard here at the Benbow Inn all of Flint's crew—all of 'em that's left——

Jim. (*Frightened*) Not Flint the Buccaneer?

Captain. Flint's crew—I was first mate—aboard that ship there—(*Points to print over mantel*) Old Flint's first mate—and I'm the only one as knows the place.

Jim. What place?

Captain. The place where Flint hid all his money—the chart's up there in my chest—Flint gave it to me in Savannah as he lay dyin'—but you won't peach, lad, 'less they get the Black Spot on me, will you, Jim?

Jim. No—no, Captain.

Captain. Or 'less you see a sea-faring man with one leg—him above all others—you'll keep your weathery-eye open, lad? (*Gets up but he is very weak*) And if I get away, I'll pay you well—if I don't—you go to that chest and you takes out the money I owes your mother—and—a little package in oilcloth—take that to the doctor—he'll tell you what to do.

Jim. (*Goes to help the* Captain *who totters toward the stairs*) Let me help you——

Captain. No. Bill Bones can stand alone—yet —and with your help, sonny, we'll beat 'em—you'll see—we'll beat 'em yet——

Jim. (*Upstairs*) Mother—mother——

Mrs. Hawkins. What is it?

Jim. Those men down there at the cove.

Mrs. Hawkins. Yes.

Jim. They—they are pirates.

Mrs. Hawkins. What?

Jim. Flint's crew. They've come for the Captain up there. (*Whistle*) Hear that?

Mrs. Hawkins. What is it?

Jim. It's a signal. (*Whistle*) There's the answer. (*Noise*) He's heard it up there.

Mrs. Hawkins. (*Crosses to* L. *of stairs*) Oh,

dear, what shall we do. They'll be about our ears. What shall we do?

JIM. We must send word to the doctor.

MRS. HAWKINS. Yes—yes—come—quick——

JIM. No. I've got to stay—my orders were to watch——

MRS. HAWKINS. But——

JIM. Dr. Livesey made me an officer of the crown and I must stay—so you must go, mother.

MRS. HAWKINS. And leave you alone, Jim—no—no—no——

JIM. The doctor is relying on us, mother.

MRS. HAWKINS. But the fog's so thick!

JIM. Just to the village, and be sure to tell the doctor they're not smugglers they're pirates—Flint's crew—quick.

MRS. HAWKINS. (*Kissing him*) Oh, Jim—Jim. You close the door—you close it tight.

JIM. There—there, mother, quick—there's no time to lose—remember—(*Exits* L. I E. *He holds the door open and calls softly*) Mother—Mother—(*When he gets no answer, he closes the door and comes back into the room. Then suddenly he gives a start for there is heard the tapping of a person with a cone. The tapping comes closer and closer and finally stops outside the door*) What's that? (*There is a slight pause.* JIM *trembles. There is a knock at the door. With a gulp* JIM *stumbles back. A second knock and* JIM *masters his fear and approaches timidly the door. He opens it. There stands a man, " plainly blind—a great green shade over his eyes and nose; he was hunched as if with age and weakness, and wore a tattered old sea-cloak with hood, and that made him appear positively deformed. His voice was an odd sing-song." He is* PEW)

PEW. (R. C.) Will any kind friend inform a poor blind man where or in what part of the country he is?

Jim. You are at the Admiral Benbow Inn, Black Hill Cove.

Pew. I hear a young voice—Will you lead me in, my kind young friend?

Jim. (*Takes* Pew *by hand*) There, sir—easy now—gently and—Oh! (*He winces with pain as* Pew's *manner suddenly changes and he finds his arm gripped tight*) You're hurting my arm, sir—not so tight.

Pew. (*Hard and menacing*) Take me to the Captain.

Jim. (*Trying to get away*) Oh, please sir—please, sir——

Pew. Take me or I'll break your arm——

Jim. The Captain is ill, sir—very ill.

Pew. Lead me straight to him and then say: "Here's a friend for you, Bill." If you don't, this instant—I'll——

Jim. (*As* Pew *has suddenly stopped to urge him and now stands listening*) Please, let me go, sir—please.

Pew. I hear someone on the stairs—unless Pew's ears trick him it's our friend the Captain—Is it? Answer! (*Squeezes* Jim's *arm*) Is it?

Jim. It is, sir.

Pew. Then remember what I said. And I'm holding on to your arm—(*He tightens his grip upon* Jim *who winces. The* Captain *comes tottering downstairs under the weight of his sea-chest. He seems very feeble*)

Captain. We'll beat 'em, yet—We'll beat 'em, yet, Jim——

Pew. (*Whispers to* Jim *and pinches*) Say it! Now!

Jim. (*Winces under* Pew's *hold*) Here—here's a friend for you, Bill.

Captain. (*Turns and sees* Pew. *At sight of him he lets the chest fall with a crash and totteringly*

supports himself against it, seeming quite dazed)
Pew!

PEW. (*To* JIM) Lead me to him. (*As* JIM *leads him up to the* CAPTAIN) Now, Bill, stay just where you are—business is business—hold out your hand—Boy, take his hand by the wrist and bring it close to mine. (JIM *does as directed and* PEW *passes a paper into the hands of the* CAPTAIN *who seems to crumple up when he receives it)* Now, that's done. Lead me to the door, Boy. (JIM *leads him to the door)* Good-day to you, Bill. (*He goes out.* JIM *comes running back to the* CAP-TAIN *who stands staring at the paper in his hand)*

JIM. (*As the* CAPTAIN *stands swaying back and forth dizzily and looking down at the paper in his hand)* What—what is it?

CAPTAIN. The Black Spot. (*Turns over the paper and reads)* Till ten o'clock—(*With increasing force as if getting an idea)* They've got me but they shan't have that chest—Flint's fist—Bill Bones is still in command. They shan't have it—they shan't—they shan't—(*He stumbles up to the door and then as he gets there with a hoarse cry he puts his arm before his eyes and stumbles back into the room. He reels, puts his hand to his throat, stands swaying a moment and then, with a peculiar sound, falls from his whole height foremost to the floor. Falls* R. *of stairs)*

JIM. (*Bends over the* CAPTAIN) Captain! Captain! (*Feels his chest)* Oh! (*With a frightened cry he starts back as* MRS. HAWKINS *enters* L. 2) Mother! (*Points to* CAPTAIN) The Captain——

MRS. HAWKINS. Dead! Glory be!

JIM. Get a candle—You sent word to the doctor? (*Starts away)*

MRS. HAWKINS. (*Holding* JIM *back)* Yes. What are you going to do?

JIM. The Captain said I was to get the money

he owes us out of his sea-chest and I'm going to do it. (*Moves towara body*)

MRS. HAWKINS. Jim! (JIM *gets key from* CAPTAIN's *hand*) Oh, Jim, don't.

JIM. Bring the candle, mother. (*Goes upstairs followed by* MRS. HAWKINS. *Off-stage*) Ah!

MRS. HAWKINS. (*Still at door*) What is it?

JIM. (*Off-stage*) A quadrant—tobacco!

MRS. HAWKINS. But the money, Jim, the money.

JIM. (*Enters on stairs*) Here it is.

MRS. HAWKINS. I'll take my due, not a penny more. What kind of money is this?

JIM. Pieces of eight. Spanish and French.

MRS. HAWKINS. Spanish and French, Jim, who was this man?

JIM. A pirate! A buccaneer. He sailed on that ship with Flint.

MRS. HAWKINS. Pirates!

JIM. All of them.

MRS. HAWKINS. Pirates' gold. Put it back. I won't touch it. Lock it up again.

JIM. All right, mother (*Exits and trunk slams. Re-enters*) It's all right. I've got it.

MRS. HAWKINS. Got what?

JIM. The package he said I was to take to the doctor.

(PEW's *taps*.)

MRS. HAWKINS. What's that?

JIM. The blind man. He was here before for the Captain.

MRS. HAWKINS. They'll be murdering us all now.

JIM. (*Drawing mother downstairs*) Come, mother. Quick! The back way!

MRS. HAWKINS. I can't; my legs won't move.

JIM. Come! Come! (*They exit. Flag-stone outside door for* PEW *to tap. Noise outside*)

PEW. (*Outside*) Down with the door if they won't open it—beat it down! (*Shouts*) Will you open—or must we break it down—(*When no answer comes*) Down with the door, then, men——

MEN. (*Without*) Aye! aye!

PEW. Down with her! (*The men batter on the door as if with a large log. Finally the door is splintered to pieces*) Aye—that's it! That's it! Now in! In with you! (*There is a shout as the men rush in.* BLACK DOG—MERRY—HANDS— O'BRIEN *followed by* PEW. *To* L. C.) Now, scatter —search everywhere—quick—Quick, I say—Well, what's the matter—why do you stop? What is it? What is it? (MERRY *and* HANDS *over body.* BLACK DOG *at steps.* ANDERSON *to fireplace* R.)

MERRY. (*Who with the other men have stumbled over* BILL *and stand eyeing him*) Bill's dead!

PEW. Well! Well!

HANDS. He's dead—done for—don't you understand, Pew?

PEW. Search him, you shirking lubbers—The chart's here, somewhere, and we are going to get it—find that chest—look for it.

BLACK DOG. It's here, Pew.

PEW. Open it quick.

BLACK DOG. It's locked!

(ANDERSON *with poker crosses to* L.)

PEW. Break it open. Smash it open! (*Chest thrown downstairs and smashed open*) Is it there? The chart?

MERRY. They've been here before us.

BLACK DOG. Someone's turned the chest alow and aloft!

HANDS. (*Who has been searching through the chest*) There's some money——

PEW. Hang the money—it's Flint's fist I want, Flint's fist——

BLACK DOG. We don't see it nowhere.

MERRY. And Bill's been overhauled already—nothin' left——

PEW. It's that boy—I wish I'd put his eyes out. That chart must be here somewhere. Scatter and look for it. (*The men dash upstairs and shout*) Look everywhere—under the tables—behind the curtains—turn everything upside down. (*The men turn over the tables, tear down the hangings, HANDS tips over the chairs and scatters over the place all the furniture. A whistle is heard*) What's that!

BLACK DOG. It's Dirk's warning. We'll have to budge, mates.

PEW. Budge, you skulk—we don't stir until we find that chart.

BLACK DOG. But that signal——

PEW. You have your hands on it—scatter and look for it. Oh, shiver my soul, if I had my eyes— (*Another whistle. HANDS rushes in and the others*) Well—well—why are you coming back?

HANDS. Twice—you heard—Dirk's called—we'd better go.

PEW. (*Stands in the doorway*) Not one of you are going to leave. Why, you fools, you have your hands on thousands and you hang a leg. You'd be rich as kings and you stand there malingering—and I to lose my chance for you. If you had the pluck of a weevil in a biscuit you'd stand your ground.

BLACK DOG. We're not going to stand here and be caught.

PEW. Nut one of you goes till you find it—or maybe you've got it. (*The whistle again and sharply*) And you're hiding it on me——

HANDS. Stand out of the way, Pew—we're going——

PEW. You're not—I believe you've got it and trying to hide it from me—Give it to me—or you don't pass—(*There is sound of horses approaching*)

Black Dog. Don't you hear them coming—those horses?

Hands. Out of the way——

Pew. Not until you give it——

Hands. Alright, then, men—at him.

(*They make a lunge at* Pew *who strikes back with his staff. They quickly overpower him and throw him into a far corner of the room. Then they rush out as the horses are heard stopping near by.* Dr. Livesey's *voice is heard giving orders without.*)

Dr. Livesey. There they go—after them.

Pew. (*Groping blindly*) Black Dog—Hands— You won't leave old Pew—you'll save your old mate—(Jim *glides in*) You'll save—who's there? Who is it? Answer?

Jim. It's I—Jim Hawkins.

Pew. You! You stole that chart—by the living thunder if I can get my hands on you I'll tear your heart out—I'll—(*Making big sweeps with his cane he rushes about*)

Jim. (*Terrified*) Help! Squire! Dr. Livesey! Help!

Pew. I'll get you, you young rat—I'll get you—

Jim. (*As* Pew *comes nearer darts out the door*) Squire! Dr. Livesey. Help—quick——!

Pew. I'll get you—I'll wring your neck—(*He rushes out the door. Then of a sudden there is the report of a pistol. There is a shriek and then* Jim *rushes into the room. Almost at once he is followed by the* Squire *and* Dr. Livesey)

Dr. Livesey. Jim, what's this story we hear about pirates?

Jim. It's true, sir.

Squire. This was Flint's crew.

Jim. Yes, sir—and that man there was Flint's mate.

Squire.   But if this is true——

Jim.   Here, sir, is the proof of it—(*Offers packet*)

Dr. Livesey.   What's this?

Jim.   I took it from his sea-chest there.   It's a map showing where Flint buried his treasure.

Squire.   What?

Dr. Livesey.   By gad, if this should be——

Squire.   Thousands upon thousands Flint buried, and hundreds have tried to find it—if this should prove the clue to Flint's treasure——

Dr. Livesey.   Tall tree—Spy-glass Mountain bearing a point to the North of N. N. E.   (Black Dog *appears*)   Skeleton Island E. S. E.   The gold is in the North Cache.

Squire.   By gad, Livesey, that's it.   We'll go to Bristol; we'll fit out a ship and we'll have that treasure if it takes a year—And Hawkins shall go with us.

Jim.   You don't mean it—To go to sea with a piping boatswain and pig-tail singing seamen—bound for an unknown island to seek buried treasure——

CURTAIN.

ACT II.

Scene 1:—*The Quay at Bristol.   The entire back of stage is taken up with a sailing vessel, tied to her pier.   Upon her side there is painted her name, " Hispaniola."   A gang-plank comes from the ship's side down to the wharf.   At right, some dusty old buildings line the side down R. 1, where there is a small inn, with the sign of a " Spy-glass" hanging from above the door. There is a bench in front of this inn and from its window hangs a cage with a parrot.   The*

*left side is taken up with a large warehouse,
down to* L. I *where there is the entrance to a
street. The center of the stage is taken up
with barrels and coils of rope and boxes.*

*When the curtain rises, three or four men
each with a box or a barrel upon his shoulders,
are starting for the ship from the wharf. They
go up the gang-plank upon the ship and then
vanish from sight. Then the stage is deserted.
From his cage the parrot calls. "Pieces of
eight!" Stand by to go about. "Pieces of
eight." Finally there comes hurriedly in from*
L. I BLACK DOG, *followed by a man.* BLACK
DOG *goes to the inn door at* R. I *and peers in
in. Within men can be seen drinking—at times
bits of song come out—a roistering scene.
Fruit girl down* L. *seated.*

BLACK DOG. (*Enters from street up* L., *goes to
window. Turns from door to his companion*) See
that man in there with one leg—hopping about on a
crutch?

MAN. Yes.

BLACK DOG. You go up to him quiet-like and
say, Silver, there's a man out there as would like to
talk to you." (*As the man starts in*) Quiet-like,
remember.

(*The man goes in.* BLACK DOG *gazes through the
window for a moment, then he goes up to the
ship and stares at her. From within the inn
there comes sound of songs and ribaldry. At
last* SILVER *appears at the door* L.)

SILVER. Who's looking for Long John, Silver?
(BLACK DOG *turns*) You! Black Dog!

BLACK DOG. A nice turn you did me—leavin' me
here at the Cove——

SILVER. (*Angrily*) And a nice turn you all did
ne—with your bungling—you and Pew and the rest

of you—lettin' a fortune slip through your fingers! (*Points inside inn, where the men are singing*) Look at 'em there! All you're good for is to come whinin' to Silver and drink his grog!

BLACK DOG. Easy there, Long John.

SILVER. Well, it's so; isn't it? Isn't it?

BLACK DOG. (*Comes up confidentially as if having something to tell*) When we all ran from that place—I got lost in the fog—(*Looks about cautiously*)

SILVER. Well?

BLACK DOG. Well, I must have run in a circle for I landed up again where I started——

SILVER. The inn?

BLACK DOG. (*Goes to him* C. *Nods*) It was dark and I crept up to the windy——

SILVER. (*Intense now*) Yes!

BLACK DOG. There was Billy Bones dead upon the floor—and at a table—three of 'em pawing over a chart——

SILVER. (*Eagerly*) Flint's fist!

BLACK DOG. Flint's fist.

SILVER. (*Tense*) Three of 'em, you say?

BLACK DOG. One was a boy—he'd got the chart and given it to the men.

SILVER. And the men?

BLACK DOG. One they called Doctor.

SILVER. And the other? The other?

BLACK DOG. He was older and looked like your country gentleman.

SILVER. (*Excitedly*) His name?

BLACK DOG. It was squire—squire something—or——

SILVER. Squire—Trelawney?

BLACK DOG. (*Astonished*) The very same!

SILVER. Ha! I guessed it! I guessed it!

BLACK DOG. But——

SILVER. (*Points to Hispaniola*) See that boat? That belongs to Squire Trelawney. (*As* BLACK

Dog *starts*) And she's sailing on sealed orders——
BLACK DOG. Then, you know——
SILVER. The squire and I have already passed the time of day—I've been watching him—I been wondering what all this is about—(*With sudden change*) That's why I have all the men in there now. Any of 'em see you down at the Cove?
BLACK DOG. None but the boy—and he saw only Pew and me.
SILVER. Good. (*Confidentially*) They haven't shipped their crew yet—I'm going to try to make our friends here take us to Flint's treasure—in their own ship—aye, even find the treasure for us—and then——
BLACK DOG. What then?
SILVER. (*Sinister*) Then we'll pay 'em for it! (TRELAWNEY *and* SMOLLETT *appear upon the ship.* SILVER *points them out to* BLACK DOG. *Turns him around*) Either one of those your squire?
BLACK DOG. Aye—the old man——
SILVER. Go inside—You'll find all the men there —but not a word!

(BLACK DOG *goes into the inn.* SILVER *wanders up the quay as* SMOLLETT *and the* SQUIRE *come down from the boat.*)

SMOLLETT. I will try, sir; but they are not so easy to get!
SQUIRE. (R. C.) My dear, Captain Smollett, there must be plenty of men——
SMOLLETT. (L. C.) But your requirements are peculiar, sir——
SQUIRE. (R. C.) What! Merely men—not afraid of anything on sea or land? Surely sir, English manhood has not gone back so far that the spirit of adventure is lost——
SMOLLETT. (L. C.) All very well, sir—but asking your pardon—I don't know the nature of this voyage,

Squire. And are not to! Sealed orders, sir——

Smollett. Quite right. But you must realize this makes it difficult to get men—honest men.

Squire. It shouldn't. England has stood for centuries for her sailors to unknown lands—and on unknown seas—her Drakes and Raleighs—and Hawkes—and——

Smollett. Very well, sir—I'll do the best I can. (*Starts away up* L.)

Squire. (*Follows him up*) And make haste, Captain—my friends come within three days—I must be ready, then——

Smollett. I'll try, sir.

(*He goes off* L. U. *The* Squire *is going toward the vessel, when* Silver *puts himself in his way.*)

Silver. (L. C. *Indicates ship*) I never tire of looking at her, sir——

Squire. (R. C.) Pretty, isn't she?

Silver. Never saw a sweeter little craft.

Squire. (*Indicates* Silver's *loss of leg*) Not a sea-faring man?

Silver. I lost that, sir, in defense of my country.

Squire. (*Drawing nearer, interested*) Did you, now?

Silver. Aye, sir, under the immortal Hawkes!

Squire. What! Not really——

Silver. A fact, sir.

Squire. Pensioned of course——

Silver. No, sir—never asked it—never needed it—I keep the Spy-glass there——

Squire. Still you should have your reward.

Silver. I have, sir. (*Salutes*) In England—my country—God bless her!

Squire. (*Enthusiastically*) A fine spirit—the true spirit of an Englishman!

Silver. There's only one thing—my health's not good ashore—having been to sea so long—that's why I keep my inn here on the quay—where I can get a bit of salt-air and meet sea-faring men—why, every sailor as comes to port knows Long John Silver——

SQUIRE. Do they now!

SILVER. They're all welcome, sir, whether they can pay or no—because of my love of her out there —the sea—(*The* SQUIRE TRELAWNEY *starts rather surprised at* SILVER) I tell you, when the sea once gets into you, sir—it's hard to ever lose her! May sound queer to you, sir—but it's a fact——

SQUIRE. (*Studying* SILVER) No—no, I think I understand——

SILVER. When I think of the times, I've seen— dirty weather and clear-fights at close quarters— hand to hand—and cutlass against cutlass—against pirate and buccaneer. (SQUIRE *starts but* SILVER *hurries on*) And then I thinks of me in there doling out grog—and, sir, it's like torture, and when I comes out here and sees a trim little schooner like that a-sailin'—why I'd give my life, sir, for just one more chance at the old sea——

SQUIRE. (*Who has been thinking and studying* SILVER) You say you know every sea-faring man in Bristol?

SILVER. Aye—sir—they all come to the Spy-glass.

SQUIRE. Well, suppose—just suppose now I wanted a special sort of crew—men not only sailors but fighters, perhaps——

SILVER. (*Points to inn*) There are men in there now—enough to man this boat—men who have sailed as I have sailed—against Flint himself. (SILVER'S *parrot begins to squawk*) Excuse me, sir—that's my parrot—I call him Captain Flint— that's why he piped up when he heard the name.

SQUIRE. You mean to say you have sailed against Flint?

SILVER. It's to him I owe the loss of this——(*In-*

dicates leg) You see, sir, that's what makes it so hard—to have been through all that and to sit idle and hear the sea calling—begging for a chance, sir— a chance that means life, sir——

SQUIRE. Suppose, now, you were offered that chance——

SILVER. You don't mean it, sir?

SQUIRE. You could help me get together a crew?

SILVER. Yes, sir——

SQUIRE. At once.

SILVER. I'll see to everything, sir. (*As the* SQUIRE *starts* SILVER *goes on quickly*) But there are honest men in there—Englishmen—ready for any purpose.

SQUIRE. I like your talk, sir—you're engaged.

SILVER. Oh, thank you, sir!

SQUIRE. And now about a crew. My captain has found difficulty——

SILVER. Might I ask, sir, what sort of voyage this is to be?

SQUIRE. (*Suspiciously*) Why?

SILVER. So I may judge about the men.

SQUIRE. I want tough men—such as you just spoke of—men willing to board Flint himself!

SILVER. I know the very men for you. They're in there now. You go to your cabin and I'll send them to you——

SQUIRE. Very well. If I could get them before Captain Smollett returns.

SILVER. I'm sure you can——

SQUIRE. I'll show him. He with his trouble about getting honest men—Send them along, Silver —(*Starts up boat*)

SILVER. Yes, sir—at once, sir—and I want to thank you, sir——

SQUIRE. (*Goes up on ship*) Not at all. Glad we met, Silver——

SILVER. It's a great thing, for me, sir—a great thing. (*The* SQUIRE *disappears in the schooner.*

Silver's *manner changes at once*) Heaven has
sent him to me. (*He hastens to the door of the inn
and calls*) Hands—Arrow—Morgan—Anderson—
Merry—all you men.

(*They all come out.*)

Black Dog. (*Next to* Silver) Was I right?
Silver. It's Flint's treasure he's after, alright.
(Hands *makes movement toward ship. There is a
slight change of manner*) I'm to engage his crew—
(*There is much astonishment and guffawing among
the crew at this*) Easy—there—you are to be that
crew—you're to go to him now—You, Arrow, are
to be mate——
Arrow. Aye, Cap'n.
Silver. Anderson, coxswain.
Anderson. Coxswain is it!
Silver. Merry, you boatswain.
Merry. My old job.
Silver. The rest of you as he pleases—he's wait-
in' in his cabin for you. Go now—quick. Act
natural—nothing suspicious. (*As they start away*)
Look innocent and—fierce! On with you! (*They
start to leave when* Silver *holds back* Black Dog
who crosses last) Wait!
Black Dog. Well?
Silver. He might recognize you.
Black Dog. I told you I saw only the boy.
Silver. We'll take no chances—You'll stay
hidden in there till we sail. (*As* Black Dog *makes
a gesture of protest, he pushes him toward the inn
door*) We've got him baited—and we'll get him—
hook and all. (*He shoves* Black Dog *into the inn
and then he goes quickly up on the ship*)
Parrot. Pieces of eight! Pieces of eight!

CURTAIN.

ACT II.

SCENE 2:—*The Quay at Bristol. The Hispaniola
ready to sail. When the curtain rises there is
a string of men going between the ship and
wharf, carrying boxes and barrels upon their
shoulders. The pirate crew. Upon the side of
the ship there stands* ISRAEL HANDS *with
bo'sain's whistle, as if directing the men. A
little farther away stands* CAPTAIN SMOLLETT
watching.

*As the men work some sing a rude sea-song,
but not the "Fifteen men on a dead man's
chest." Others are shouting and talking excitedly; about the whole scene there is an air of
excitement and noise.*

HANDS.   (*As the last man comes up the plank*)
That all?
ANDERSON.   (*Comes aboard with a box*) Aye,
aye, sir.
MORGAN.   That's all of it.

(HANDS *turns to* SMOLLETT *and salutes.*)

HANDS.   Captain Smollett——
SMOLLETT.   (*Upper deck*) Well, Mr. Hands?
HANDS.   (*Below deck*) Everything right, sir?
SMOLLETT.   Sure you've missed nothing?
HANDS.   Sure, sir.
SMOLLETT.   All ready to cast off?
HANDS.   All sir—all ready—Shall I give the
word, sir?

(BLACK DOG *enters.*)

SMOLLETT.   Squire Trelawney is not here yet—
Have all the men stand by.
HANDS.   Aye—aye, sir.

SMOLLETT. Mr. Hands?

HANDS. Yes, sir.

SMOLLETT. (*With change*) Who gave you the orders for the stowing of those stores?

HANDS. I thought you did, sir!

SMOLLETT. (*Dismissing him*) Very well.

HANDS. Aye, aye, sir. (*Goes out. For a moment* SMOLLETT *stands as if thinking and then he turns as if to follow* HANDS. *Meanwhile* BLACK DOG *has sneaked upon the scene and is slinking up the gang-plank when* SMOLLETT *turns and sees him*)

SMOLLETT. Well, my man? Who are you?

BLACK DOG. (*On gang-plank*) A—A friend of one of the crew, sir—I have a message.

SMOLLETT. This boat is ready to sail—no one boards her now.

BLACK DOG. But, sir, it's important—most important I see him.

SMOLLETT. Who?

BLACK DOG. Silver, sir. Long John Silver.

SMOLLETT. (*Calls*) Silver! John Silver!

SILVER. (*Without*) Aye, sir.

SMOLLETT. Man to see you.

SILVER. (*Coming*) Coming sir, coming—What is it, sir? (*Sees* BLACK DOG *and starts*)

SMOLLETT. This fellow here says he has a message for you.

SILVER. (*Recovering himself and feigning surprise*) A message for me, my good man?

BLACK DOG. Aye——

SILVER. (*Noticing that* SMOLLETT *is watching and that* BLACK DOG *is growing embarrassed*) Well—well—speak up, my man.

BLACK DOG. (*Indicates inn*) There's someone there as would like to talk to you. He said it was most important. (*Crosses L.*)

SILVER. (*To* SMOLLETT) I don't know who it could be, nor what he wants—Can I go ashore, sir?

SMOLLETT. We're already to cast off.

SILVER. I won't be but a jiffy, sir.

SMOLLETT. Very well. (*Goes out*)

SILVER. Thank you, sir. (*Comes down with* BLACK DOG *and turns fiercely upon him* L.) By all the powers what are you tryin' to do?

BLACK DOG. That boat's sailin'?

SILVER. Well?

BLACK DOG. It'll never sail without me! If I don't go—I'll blow the whole thing. (*As* SILVER *starts to threaten him*) I will. I'm going. You hear?

SILVER. You'll do as I say—(HANDS *comes rushing down.* SILVER *crosses to gang-plank*) How now, Hands? (*Stage* R.)

HANDS. That Captain Smollett.

SILVER. What's he done?

HANDS. He's down below snooping around——

SILVER. You put the powder where I told you?

HANDS. Aye.

SILVER. And their men—bunked with ours?

HANDS. Aye.

SILVER. Did he notice it?

HANDS. I don't know—he acts suspicious-like.

SILVER. (*Turns angrily on* BLACK DOG) You hear that, Black Dog—you hear? Now you go inside there and wait. Go, I say, or by thunder, I'll run you through.

BLACK DOG. (*Driven to the inn door*) You'll never go without me—never!

SILVER. Go! (BLACK DOG *goes in.* SILVER *storms*) Luck never came with that man. (*Suddenly*) Hands, Black Dog doesn't go on this criuse.

HANDS. Aye—aye.

SILVER. (*As* SQUIRE *and* DR. LIVESEY *come from street* L. U.) Go inside there—Watch him, don't leave him out of your sight, and wait your chance and when you get it you know what to do.

(*Stiletto bus.* HANDS *goes in as* DR. LIVESEY *and* SQUIRE *come down*)

HANDS. Aye, aye, sir. (*Exits into door of Inn*)

SQUIRE. I don't know what to make of it.

DR. LIVESEY. I'm sure he'll come, Squire.

SILVER. (*Comes forward*) Everything ready and ship-shape—Just waiting for you, sir——

SQUIRE. (*Testily*) Hawkins hasn't come——

DR. LIVESEY. You told him he might stay till the last minute with his mother.

SILVER. If we wait—we'll miss the tide. That means another twelve hours delay, sir.

SQUIRE. (*Excitedly*) Look at her there! Everything ready and to be held up now—by Gad, it's hard, sir.

SILVER. (*Parrot*) Would you mind if I took my old shipmate, Captain Flint, with us—he goes on all my voyages with me. (*Starts away and then stops*) Oh, perhaps you gentlemen would join us— in a glass of grog, or——

SQUIRE. Thank you, Silver, but if you'll excuse me.

SILVER. Certainly, sir.—I understand, sir. (*Goes in*)

SQUIRE. An honest fellow and capable.

DR. LIVESEY. Well, Squire, I don't usually put much faith in your discoveries, but John Silver suits me. (*Start for boat*)

SQUIRE. (*Crosses* R.) The man's a perfect trump—We've grown quite familiar.

DR. LIVESEY. Squire, you haven't told him any- thing——

SQUIRE. Not a word. I have been most discreet. On the contrary—I've got all his simple little secrets from him. (*As they start for the boat*) He leaves a wife to manage his inn——

DR. LIVESEY. Indeed?

SQUIRE. A lady of colour.

DR. LIVESEY. No!

(*They laugh and go up into the boat. Enter* JIM
L. U. *with bundle. Goes to Inn and knocks.*)

SILVER. Well, my lad?
JIM. Silver—Mr. Silver—I'm looking for——
SILVER. That's my name, lad—and who may
you be?
JIM. (*Hands* SILVER *a letter.* C.) Hawkins,
sir.
SILVER. (R. C. *Crosses to* R.) Oh, I see. You
are our new cabin boy. Pleased I am to ʿʾe you.
We've been waiting for you.

(*There is a sound of commotion within the inn.*)

JIM. (L. C. *of window*) Oh, sir—what's that?
SILVER. (R. C. *of window, puts* JIM *behind him.
Trying to cover the noise*) Oh, that—that's noth-
ing, lad—just some men drinking there in my
house.
JIM. I think it's a fight!

(BLACK DOG *pursued by* HANDS *appears at the
door.*)

BLACK DOG. I know my rights and you can't
stop me. I'd fight the whole crew of you. (*Exit*
L. U.)
JIM. (*Suddenly recognizes* BLACK DOG. *Cries
out. Points excitedly to* BLACK DOG) Why, it's
Black Dog! (SILVER *puts him* R.) Stop him, sir—
stop him.
SILVER. Hands! After that man—quick.

(HANDS *rushes out* L.

JIM. (R.) It was Black Dog. I'm sure of it.
SILVER. (R. C.) I don't care two coppers who
he is. He hasn't paid his score. What did you say
his name was? Black what?

JIM. Black Dog, sir. Hasn't Mr. Trelawney told you of the buccaneers?

SILVER. What?

JIM. He was one of them, sir.

SILVER. So! One of those swabs—In my house! (*As* HANDS *returns. Comes on from street* L. U.) Well?

HANDS. He got away, sir.

SILVER. (*Meaningly*) You know who that was, Hands?

HANDS. No, sir.

SILVER. (*With meaning*) Black Dog. Isn't it so, Hawkins?

JIM. Yes, sir.

SILVER. And do you know who Black Dog is?

HANDS. No, sir.

SILVER. One of Flint's crew. (*As* HANDS *starts*) Now, Hands, you was drinking with him in there. Aye—That's who you've let go—Now aboard with you and be a little more particular who you consort with hereafter. (HANDS *exits ship*) Now, see here, Hawkins; this is a blessed hard thing on a man like me. There's Squire Trelawney —what's he to think? Here I have this confounded son of a Dutchman sitting in my own house, drinking my own rum—Here you comes and tells me of it plain and I let him give us the slip before my blessed dead-lights.

JIM. It wasn't your fault.

SILVER. Nay, that it wasn't—but it might look so.

JIM. I'll explain it to the Squire.

SILVER. Will you, now?

JIM. Just as soon as I see them.

SILVER. (*Anxiously*) No—no—lad you wait till we sail—and then when he sees how I work and knows me better—then you ups and tells him— and he'll understand.

JIM. Very well, sir.

SILVER. There's a lad for you—and—(*Stops suddenly and breaks out into a laugh*) Why, what a precious old sea-calf I am.

JIM. What is it, sir?

SILVER. That swab got away without paying his score—three goes of rum—Shiver my timbers if I hadn't forgotten my score. (*Falls on a bench laughing*) Dash my buttons but that's a good 'un about my score.

(*As they laugh* SQUIRE *and* DR. LIVESEY *comes down from ship.*)

DR. LIVESEY. Jim, my lad, we've been anxious about you.

SQUIRE. (R. C.) Where have you been?

JIM. It was mother kept me, sir—she's so afraid —and she's quite alone.

SQUIRE. I sent her a boy to take your place——

JIM. Yes, sir, and very kind it was—only—he can't take my place, sir.

DR. LIVESEY. That's conceit for you, Squire.

JIM. (*Crosses to* DR. LIVESEY R.) Oh, no—no, sir—you see there is just mother and me now—and —(*Breaking*) We've never been parted before— (*Cries*)

DR. LIVESEY. (*Comes up and pets* JIM) There —there—Jim. I understand—of course.

SILVER. (*Significantly to the* SQUIRE) Begging your pardon, sir—don't you think it might be good if I took him on board, sir?

JIM. (*Mastering himself*) Oh, I'm alright, sir —I'm alright.

SILVER. (*Crosses* R. *to* JIM) Come with me, lad —Silver will show you your quarters. (*Leads him up gang-plank*)

SQUIRE. (R. DR. LIVESEY *crosses to* L. C.) And now, the ship's company is complete—and (CAPTAIN SMOLLETT *comes hurrying down*) Well, sir, already to sail? We mustn't miss this tide, sir.

SMOLLETT. (R.) Squire Trelawney—I don't like this criuse and I don't like my crew.

SQUIRE. (R. C. *startled*) Eh?

SMOLLETT. I was engaged to sail this ship undei sealed orders.

SQUIRE. Right.

SMOLLETT. Then if that is so, how is it every man before the mast knows more than I do.

DR. LIVESEY. (C.) Squire!

SQUIRE. That's not true!

SMOLLETT. (*Meaningly*) I learn we are going after treasure—Now, treasure is ticklish work and I don't like treasure voyages on any account—but when they're secret and the secret's been blabbed

———

SQUIRE. Blabbed!

SMOLLETT. Yes, sir, blabbed—Why, sir, it's life or death and a close run.

SQUIRE. If you're afraid.

DR. LIVESEY. (*Holding back* SQUIRE) Squire! (*To* SMOLLETT. SQUIRE *crosses 2 to apple stand*) You say you don't like the crew—aren't they good seamen?

SQUIRE. (*Goes to apple stand*) I dare him to deny that.

SMOLLETT. Six of the men I chose were discharged.

SQUIRE. They were fresh water swabs. Silver showed me that. (*Crosses to box—sits*)

SMOLLETT. And do you think it fair that this Silver—the ship's cook—should have had more authority than I in choosing my own crew?

SQUIRE. It was a chance to get men quickly.

SMOLLETT. A slur on me, sir——

DR. LIVESEY. (*As* SQUIRE *is about to reply*) Captain Smollett. Just what are you aiming at? Come.

SMOLLETT. (*With sudden determination*) You gentlemen know the risks you're running?

SQUIRE. We do.

SMOLLETT. And you are determined to go?

SQUIRE. We are.

SMOLLETT. Then I have this to say. Without my orders those men put all the powder and arms in the forehold—there's a place under our cabin—why not put them there?

SQUIRE. But——

DR. LIVESEY. (*Stopping the* SQUIRE) Alright, Captain. What else?

SMOLLETT. You have some of your people with you——

SQUIRE. You don't doubt them, too?

SMOLLETT. Berth them beside the cabin.

DR. LIVESEY. (*Intercepting the* SQUIRE *as he again starts to answer*) Go on, Captain Smollett.

SMOLLETT. (*Meaningly*) I've heard you have a certain chart—that there are crosses on that chart.

SQUIRE. (*Rises. Startled*) I never told that to a soul.

SMOLLETT. Every man aboard knows it, sir——

SQUIRE. Then Livesey it must have been you

——

SMOLLETT. I don't know who has this chart and I don't want to know—but I insist it be kept secret.

DR. LIVESEY. In short you fear a mutiny?

SMOLLETT. I deny your right, sir, to put those words into my mouth. No Captain would be justified in going to sea if he had ground to say that.

SQUIRE. What then?

SMOLLETT. Some of these men may be honest—perhaps all are. But I am responsible for the ship's safety and the life of every man Jack aboard her and I demand that I be allowed to take these precautions—or I resign!

SQUIRE. Well then (*Angrily*) You can——

DR. LIVESEY (*To* SQUIRE) Wait. I agree with

Captain Smollett. I think it wise to do as Captain Smollett says.

SQUIRE. (*Crosses* R. C. *to* SMOLLETT) Very well, then—I am overruled. (*Turns to* CAPTAIN) But let me tell you I think the worse of you, Captain Smollett, but do as you wish.

SMOLLETT. Thank you, sir. As soon as we are under way I'll give orders for the removal of the arms from the forehold. (CAPTAIN *goes to his position on the boat*)

SQUIRE. (*As he and* DR. LIVESEY *follow*) I should have sent him packing.

DR. LIVESEY. Squire, I think you have two honest men aboard. Captain Smollett and John Silver.

SMOLLETT. (*On the boat*) Boatswain, ahoy! (*Boatswain blows*) Pipe all hands.

(*Enter* CREW.)

MERRY. Aye, aye, sir.

SQUIRE. Doesn't it set you all atingle, Livesey?

SMOLLETT. Top-man aloft.

MORGAN *and* O'BRIEN. Aye, aye, sir.

SQUIRE. (*Coming up to top of gang-plank*) Off at last, Livesey.

SMOLLETT. Loose your top-gallant—(JOYCE *and* RED)

JOYCE *and* RED. Aye, aye, sir.

SQUIRE. Seaward Ho—hang the treasure——

DR. LIVESEY. (*At foot of gang-plank*) Squire —Squire——

SQUIRE. It's the glory of the sea that's turned my head.

(DR. LIVESEY *and* SQUIRE *go on ship.*)

SMOLLETT. Cast off your gang-plank.

HUNTER *and* GRAY. Aye, aye, sir.

SMOLLETT. Haul on your main sheet——

HANDS. Aye, aye, sir.

(CREW *does so and starts to sing " Fifteen Men."* BLACK DOG *enters from street and sneaks aboard.* SQUIRE *has gone up on bridge.*)

DR. LIVESEY. Jim—Jim—Is Jim aboard?

(JIM *dashes out from among the pirates.*)

JIM. Here, Doctor.
SMOLLETT. Cast off your hawser forward——
JIM. We're starting, sir—we're starting—(JIM *turns towards pirates*)
SQUIRE. Livesey! (DOCTOR *goes to* SQUIRE)
JIM. (*Turns from pirates*) That was the song the Captain used to sing—The Pirates song—

(BUS. *until*)

CURTAIN.

——————

ACT II.

SCENE 3:—*The Hispaniola at anchor close to " Treasure Island." The part of ship shown is some of the stern and most of the amidships, the main part of the stage being taken up with what is called the " waist " of the ship. Upon the right, however, there is seen a small portion of the poop, with small brass cannon mounted upon it. In the background there can be seen a vague outline of " Treasure Island " with Spyglass Mountain glowing in the moonlight.*

When the curtain rises the men are discovered in with TRELAWNEY, SMOLLETT *and* DR. LIVESEY. *Others of the men are along the rail, some even in the rigging.*

SMOLLETT. (*On upper deck and using his hands as megaphone*) All fast there, forrard? (*Folding up chart, etc.*)

DIRK. (*Extreme* L.) All fast, sir——

SMOLLETT. Anchorage good?

DIRK. Aye, aye, sir.

SMOLLETT. The current's pretty strong here——How she's holding——

DIRK. Firm in over seven fathom, sir—-She'sn't dragged an inch!

SMOLLETT. Good! (*Turns to* CREW *in waist*) My lads, that Island there is the place we've been sailing to. (*Murmurs of satisfaction among* CREW, *etc.*) Squire Trelawney has a word to say——

SQUIRE. (*Coming forward* R. C.) Captain Smollett has told me how every man of you has done his duty alow and aloft as I never ask to see it better done; and so, to show my appreciation, I have had Silver here make ready a special mess—and double grog below decks!

SILVER. (*As the* CREW *gives a shout*) My lads, I hold this handsome, and, if you think as I do, you'll give good sea cheer for Squire Trelawney. (*As the* CREW *cheer*) Come, now, below and we'll drink a health to these gentlemen. Below——

(ALL *go off with talking and gesticulating* L.)

SQUIRE. (R. C. *Coming down*) Well, Captain Smollett, you'll admit now you were wrong.

SMOLLETT. (C.) How so, sir?

SQUIRE. A splendid voyage—a fine brisk crew—and here we are!

SMOLLETT. Aye, sir, here we are—but we're not home again.

SQUIRE. (*Testily*) By heavens, there's no pleasing you. I'm going below. (*As he goes out* R.) A trifle more of that man and I should explode. (*To* DR. LIVESEY) Yes, sir? Have you seen nothing suspicious?

DR. LIVESEY. Yes—much (R.)

SMOLLETT. Then——?

DR. LIVESEY. I believe you're right.

SMOLLETT. I tell you this crew is on the verge of mutiny—and—(*Stops short as he sees* HANDS *come from men's quarters*) What is it, Mr. Hands?

HANDS. Some of the men didn't report to mess, sir—just looking for 'em, sir—(*As* SMOLLETT *watches him keenly*) Haven't seen 'em 'bout deck, sir, have you?

SMOLLETT. Not a soul, Hands.

HANDS. Thank you, sir—(*Exits to upper deck where he continues his search; now and then looking surreptitiously at* DR. LIVESEY *and* SMOLLETT *who watch him. His actions are suspicious*)

DR. LIVESEY. You see that?

SMOLLETT. There's something in the air. We'll hear from that crew before the night's over——

DR. LIVESEY. I believe you're right.

SMOLLETT.. Then we must take some precautions —Squire or no Squire——

DR. LIVESEY. Come below—We must make the Squire listen to reason.

(*They go out. They have scarcely gone when* BLACK DOG *steals in* L. *He makes over toward the cabin when he is met by* HANDS *who comes from upper deck.*)

HANDS. Where you going?

BLACK DOG. Down to that cabin—and if I find that boy——

HANDS. You're not—You're going below——

BLACK DOG. Stand out of my way.

HANDS. You heard Silver's orders——

BLACK DOG. Aye, I've heard his orders and I've heard his talk and—(HANDS *whistles*) So—you've signalled for him—Shiver my timbers—but you'll pay for that. (*Springs at* HANDS *and they struggle*

pantingly without words. As they do so, JIM, *who
has been in the rigging but up so high that he is
out of sight, now comes slowly down. It is evident that he has heard and now he watches the
fight. He comes slyly down and is making toward
the cabin as if to go to tell the* CAPTAIN, *when he is
startled by someone approaching. In fright he
turns to hide. He sees the apple-barrel and jumps
into it as* MERRY *comes rushing in*)

MERRY. (*Trying to separate the men*) Here—
Black Dog—Hands.

(SILVER *and the rest of the men come rushing on
deck.*)

SILVER. What's all this—Put up those knives!

MERRY. I found these two trying to carve each
other up. (*The men are pulled apart.* HANDS L.
and BLACK DOG C.)

HANDS. I caught him making for the cabin.

SILVER. (*To* BLACK DOG) You heard my
orders——

BLACK DOG. The men are back of me in this

———

SILVER. Are they? Well; who's Cap'n here, I'd
like to know. By thunder I'll show you—the whole
pack of you—Give me that knife—Give it to me—
(BLACK DOG *gives up his knife and* SILVER *turns to*
HANDS) Here, Hands, I place him in your charge
—at the first word—the first sign—you kill him.
Understand—kill him.

BLACK DOG. (*As he goes off with* HANDS) I'll
pay you for this, Long John—If he touches me I'll
tear him to pieces. (*Out* L.)

(SILVER *turns to the men who are in groups.*)

MORGAN. (R C.) John, John—we want to——
SILVER. (*Stopping him*) Wait. (*Indicates*

cabin and the men look stealthily to see if anyone is about)

MORGAN. (R.) All clear——

(*Others murmur the same or " no one here,"—etc.*)

SILVER. Now then—out with it.

MORGAN. We men want to know how long we're going to hold off?

SILVER. By the powers till the last minute I can manage—(*As the men make an angry start*) They've got that chart and until we have it—we make no move——

MERRY. And didn't we see it this very night here in their hands. If you had let us at 'em then——

SILVER. And you think they'll sit still and let you cut their throats while doing it, eh?

DIRK. We're nineteen to six and——

MERRY. We've taken a vote.

SILVER. Oh, have you now?

MERRY. We know our rights, Long John.

SILVER. Another word, George Merry, and——

MERRY. Fo'c's'le council, Long John. Them's rules—rules——

SILVER. Rules is it—I'll show ye rules—you'll have all the rules you want—(*Sounds of fighting in foc'sle. Stops suddenly*) What's that?

ANDERSON. It's Hands and Black Dog

SILVER. Stop 'em—stop 'em, quick. Below with you all. Quick. Here comes the Doctor. If the Squire hears that rumpus we'll be ditched. Quick. Don't let them see anything.

(*As the men rush out* DR. LIVESEY *and* SQUIRE *and* SMOLLETT *come in.*)

SMOLLETT. What was that noise, Silver?

SILVER. (*Innocently*) Noise, sir? I didn't notice anything. If there's anything wrong I'll soon settle it—you can trust me, sir. (*Goes out quickly*)

SQUIRE. Of course I trust you. It's only ridiculous trouble-seekers who do not. It's——

JIM. You're wrong, sir—(*Turns to* DR. LIVESEY) Oh, sir, I have been in there and I heard—it's mutiny, sir—and talk about treasure and falling on us to get our chart—sir——

SQUIRE. What's that?

JIM. Yes, it's Silver, sir—He's the sea-faring man with one leg that sailed with Flint—they are pirates—Flint's crew—they know what we were after—and they've used us—to get their ship and sail it for them to the very treasure place——

SMOLLETT. That's it! That explains everything—(*Turns on* SQUIRE) Squire, you trusted (*Crosses to* L. C.) Silver——

SQUIRE. I did.

SMOLLETT. And Silver got it from you——

DR. LIVESEY. (*To* SQUIRE) Are you convinced now, Squire?

SQUIRE. Captain, you were right. I was wrong. I own myself an ass and await orders.

SMOLLETT. (*To* JIM) Did you here anything of their plans——

JIM. They're arguing down there now. The men are all for attack—but Silver is all for holding them back. If he only——

SMOLLETT. If he only could. How many men can we count on?

JIM. They said they were nineteen to six.

SMOLLETT. Six—that must be Rudruth—Joyce —Hunter and ourselves.

DR. LIVESEY. Then there are some who are doubtful——

SMOLLET. Well, count on six—Ammunition and arms with us. By Gad, if Silver can only hold them off—if we can get a little time. This ship needs water. Without it, she can't sail—Now, according to your chart, there is just one place on that Island where water can be had—The stockade. Now if we can make the stockade with our arms and provisions, by heaven, sir, they'd have to come to us—if we could only hold them off for a time— (Joyce *rushes in*) How now, Joyce?

(Joyce *by door*.)

Joyce. Begging your pardon, sir, but there's things come over that crew——

Smollett. Go on!

Joyce. First they tried to make Redruth and Hunter and me join 'em and when we refused they shut themselves in a corner by themselves——

Smollett. Well?

Joyce. I stole back and listened—it's all about a chart, sir—and they're coming to demand it.

Squire. Good Lord!

Joyce. Silver's been trying to hold 'em back, sir —but—I'm afraid if they don't get it, sir—why— it's mutiny, sir—and—death.

Squire. What shall we do? Captain Smollett?

Jim. I beg your pardon, sir. You say it's time you want.

Smollett. Yes—yes——

Jim. Well, then, why not give them the map, sir?

Dr. Livesey. What?

Jim. They think the map that Captain Smollett has to sail the ship by is the right one—Couldn't we give them that?

Smollett. Jim, I think you've hit it. (*Turns to* Squire) That map you gave me was a true one except for the crosses where the treasure is buried.

Squire. It was.

Smollett. Jim, you'll find that chart down in my cabin—take it—put some crosses on—put them anywhere—Understand?

Jim. Yes, sir.

Smollett. Then bring it up here and slip it into the Squire's hand—Hurry. (Jim *rushes out*)

Dr. Livesey. I believe the lad has solved it.

Smollett. (*Turns to* Dr. Livesey *and* Squire) Now, in case this comes to an issue, are you gentlemen willing to fight them?

Dr. Livesey. To the last, sir——

Squire. Aye, sir.

Smollett. Very well. Have your pistols primed.

Squire. They are, sir.

Dr. Livesey. And mine, sir.

Smollett. Joyce, as soon as those men come from below take all the muskets and load them—drag as much powder and shot into the cabin as you can——

Joyce. Very well, sir.

Smollett. Stand there on guard. Let no one touch it.

Joyce. Right, sir.

Smollett. If it comes to a fight, we'll fight back to the cabin and the ammunition—we've got a chance, gentlemen—just a bare chance—and if we don't make it, we'll sell our lives dear—Steady now! Steady all. (*The pirates led by* Silver *come forward in an angry group.* Silver, *however, is apparently trying to cover his face somewhat*) Well, my men, this looks like a deputation.

Silver. It is, sir—a deputation.

Smollett. (*Sternly*) Well, what is it?

Silver. (*Hesitates*) These men, sir—these men, sir, have been hearing rumors.

Smollett. Rumors?

Silver. Rumors, sir, as how this ship was under sealed orders—and them sealed orders are—treasure, sir!

The Men. Aye, aye—Treasure!

Squire. And who told you that?

Silver. You did, sir——

Squire. I!

Silver. Aye, sir. Now, such things getting to the ears of the men makes them sort of greedy, sir —and——

Smollett. Do you mean to say, that this is mutiny?

Silver. You can call it what you want, sir.

Smollett. Why, damme, I'll have you put in irons—I'll——

Silver. (*As the men with ugly threats go toward* Smollett—*speaks to* Squire) I think you'd better know, sir—I've counseled—peace—and fair terms.

Smollett. Well?

Silver. (*To* Squire *always*) We are told that you have a certain chart. (*The* Crew *draws nearer in a threatening manner*) With certain crosses on it—we want that chart.

Squire. Silver, I've trusted you.

Silver. The chart, sir—do we get it—do we?

Smollett. (*As* Squire *goes to answer*) Wait. Suppose we give this chart to you. What then?

Silver. What then?

Smollett. Aye, what then? What happens to us?

Silver. Why—why—nothing, sir.

Smollett. You mean you'll not harm us?

Silver. No——

Smollett. Your solemn promise?

Silver. Solemn promise.

Smollett. (*To the men*) You—you mean— you hear—you give your word, too? (*Cries of aye, aye*) Very well, then—much as I think you are a pack of scoundrels and hope to see you all hanged—(*The men come threateningly at him*) Why—I know when I'm beaten—Squire, get the chart.

Squire. Very well.

SILVER. (*As* SQUIRE *starts out*) Wait. I'll send a man with you.

SQUIRE. No need. (*Calls*) Jim!

JIM. (*Without*) Yes, sir?

SQUIRE. (*Calls*) You know where that chart is, Jim?

JIM. (*Without*) Yes, sir.

SQUIRE. (*Calls*) Bring it here.

JIM. (*Without*) In a jiffy, sir.

SILVER. (*As the men press forward*) Now then, ready with the boats, men—quick—get them ready—(*As men get to work lowering the boats*) I'll stand guard and watch—for I tell you I can't trust you, Captain Smollett.

(SMOLLETT *down* L.)

SMOLLETT. Well, I can't say as I trust you either, Silver. (*As* JIM *comes in with chart.* SILVER *rushes forward*) Wait! Remember your promise?

SILVER. Aye——

SMOLLETT. Then let them have it, Jim.

(*As* JIM *gives* SILVER *the map all the men with a cry spring forward.*)

ARROW. Now then, pals, settle with them.

SMOLLETT. Back! Back! (SQUIRE, *and* DR. LIVESEY *and* SMOLLETT *all draw their guns*) Your promise—by heavens gentlemen, if you come a step farther——

SILVER. (*Turns to the men*) Stop! Stop! I say! You fools, you blockheads——

ARROW. Well, haven't we got the chart——

SILVER. That was Flint's crew—I've seen Flint's ship amuck with blood and fit to sink with gold— aye—gold that's buried there—gold that's ours by rights—belongs to us—who have sailed with Flint

—Flint **was** Cap'n—You may as well know. I was quartermaster. (*As he sees the men again threatening he goes closer to* SMOLLETT *and speaks low*) They're a rough lot—there—it's all I can do to hold 'em. You'd better go below—quick—go!

SMOLLETT. I warn you!

SILVER. Go. (*As soon as* SMOLLETT *and* SQUIRE *and* DOCTOR *go, the men all make a dash as if they would follow them*)

MERRY. Now then, men, after them—we'll finish this up.

SILVER. Wait!

MERRY. Haven't we got the chart—haven't we

———

SILVER. Yes—and we got it too easy.

MORGAN. Too easy——

SILVER. It don't look nat'ral—there's something behind it——

DIRK. A trick—maybe a wrong chart.

MERRY. Then we'll find out soon enough—Come, lads—come (*Starts* R., *all*)

JIM. (*Stepping forward* L.) Wait.

(*The men, surprised, stop.*)

JIM. It was I got the chart from Billy Bones. I brought it from the Captain's cabin—I ought to know whether it's the right one. You go down there and attack and you'll lose everything—they're waiting for you—their muskets and pistols primed —they've got all the guns and ammunition—you go and you'll lose your ship—your chart and your lives

———

SILVER. You say this is the right chart. We'll let you risk your life on't—I mean we'll take you along as a hostage. (*As* JIM *starts*) That makes you start, eh?

JIM. (*Recovering himself*) I'm willing to go.

SILVER. Alright, we'll see. (*Calls to* HANDS) Hands——

HANDS. (R. C.) Aye—aye—sir——
SILVER. (HANDS and O'BRIEN come forward)
Hands—you and O'Brien will stay here to watch
the ship. At the first sign of anything——you fire
and tell the Squire from me that shot from this
boat will be a signal for Hawkins' death.
JIM. And tell the Squire from me that Jim Hawkins isn't afraid.
SILVER. In with him. Toss him in——(*As they
toss him in*) Now then, over with you all——(*As
the men scramble on the boats*) Push them off.
(*Gets over the side and can be heard calling*)
Away with them——

(*There are shouts and cries as the men push off.
HANDS and O'BRIEN crowd the rail, staring
after the boats. Then slowly and cautiously,
with muskets raised, there come upon the deck,
SQUIRE, SMOLLETT, DR. LIVESEY, REDRUTH,
HUNTER and JOYCE and GRAY. When HANDS
and O'BRIEN turn they confront the muskets.*)

SMOLLETT. Up with your hands. Up with them.
HANDS. What's this?
SMOLLETT. Joyce, take away their guns.
JOYCE. (*Going to men and taking guns*) Yes,
sir——
HANDS. (*Starting to lower his hands*) But——
SMOLLETT. Up with them, I say——
HANDS. Now, I warn you—you fire—you just
fire one shot and it means the death of Hawkins

DR. LIVESEY. What's that?
HANDS. They've taken him with them. I was
to tell you—that the first shot from this boat—is a
signal for his death.
DR. LIVESEY, JIM and SQUIRE. What!
SMOLLETT. Come, Livesey, to the boat.
HANDS. Where are you going?

SMOLLETT. Going! By all the stars we're going to rescue that boy—you men did just what we wanted you to—we've tricked you and we're going to fight you to the end—and I tell you this much and you can tell Silver. God help you all if anything happens to that boy.

CURTAIN.

ACT III.

SCENE 1:—*In front of* BEN GUNN'S *Cave. When the curtain rises the stage is in darkness. The darkness just before dawn. Then gradually the light comes stealing in, turning the black to gray and until this melts into tones of early dawn. The whole reaching a sort of climatic effulgence with the rise of the sun. Birds and morning fowl are heard in the trees. The whistle of insects which always ushers in dawn. The call of here and there an animal. There is no sign of anything human. The whole atmosphere of the scene suggesting a place in its primal beauty. Then, suddenly, when the sun has fully risen above the horizon, from the side of the hill which was here steep and stony a spout of gravel is dislodged and falls rattling and bounding through the trees. The next instant comes half creeping, half sliding from his cave, BEN GUNN, almost cannibal-like. He looks about hurriedly and then reassured crawls up to a crevice in the rocks from which there trickles a small stream of water. Lying full length upon the ground drinks. Then of a sudden he starts as if he heard something. Again reassured, he again stoops to drink. But this time he arises hurriedly and with more decision. He goes quickly to the left and peers through the trees. Apparently seeing no one he goes to the right and searches there. Then suddenly with a half-smothered cry, he turns, runs up back and hides. JIM enters almost at once. For a moment he looks about wonderingly. He seems weary and tired and he is about to go on when suddenly he catches sight of BEN GUNN hiding. All alert now, he stops. "My eyes turned instinctively in that direction and I saw a figure leap with great rapidity behind the trunk of a pine. What it was, whether a bear, or man or monkey, I could in nowise tell. It seemed dark and shaggy. More I knew not. But the terror of this new apparition brought me to a stand. I was now, it seemed, cut off upon both sides. Behind me the murderers, before me this lurking mondescript, and immediately I began to prefer the dangers I knew to those I knew not. SILVER himself appeared less terrible in contrast with this creature of the woods and I turned on my heel, looking sharply behind me over my shoulder, and began to retrace my steps in the direction of the boats. Instantly the figure reappeared and, making a wide circle, began to head me off. I was tired, at any rate, but had I been as fresh as when I arose, I could see it was in vain for me to contend in speed with such an advisory. From trunk to trunk the creature flitted like a deer running manlike on two legs, but unlike any man that I had ever seen, stooping almost double as it ran. Yet a man it was. I could no longer be in doubt about that. I began to recall what I had heard of cannibals. I was within an ace of calling for help, but the mere fact that he was a man however wild, had somewhat reassured me, and* **my fear of** Silver *began to revive in proportion. I stood still therefore and cast about for some method of escape. And as I was so thinking the recollection of my pistol flashed into my mind. As soon as I remembered I was not defenseless, courage glowed again in my heart and I set my face resolutely for this man of the island and walked briskly toward him. He was concealed by this time behind another tree trunk, but he must have been watching me closely for as soon as I began to move in his direction he reappeared and took a step to meet me. Then he hesitated, drew back, came forward again and at last, to my wonder and confusion, threw himself on his knees and held out his clasped hands in supplication."*

Jim. Who are you?

Gunn. Ben Gunn—I'm poor Ben Gunn, I am—and I haven't spoke with a Christian these three years.

Jim. Three years?

Gunn. Aye—three blessed years——

Jim. Shipwrecked here?

Gunn. Nay, make—marooned.

Jim. (*Startled*) Marooned! You mean—put here purposely—and left, alone—to live or die——

Gunn. Aye, mate, marooned—three years agone—and lived on goats since then and berries and oysters. Wherever man is, says I, man can do for hissel. But, mate, my heart is more for Christian diet. (*Confidentially, stepped to* Jim) Now, you mightn't have a piece of cheese about you, eh? (Jim *shakes head*) No? Well—ah! Many's the long night I've dreamed of cheese—toasted—mostly and wake up again and here I were.

Jim. If I get on board again you shall have it by the ton.

Gunn. If ever ye get on board again, says you?
(*Looking toward sea*)

Jim. Yes.

Gunn. (*Eagerly*) Why now, who's to hinder
you?

Jim. (*Noticing* Gunn's *manner and putting on
a show of bravery*) Not you, I know.

Gunn. Right you was. Now you—what do you
call yourself, mate?

Jim. Jim.

Gunn. Jim—Jim—(*Suddenly takes hold of*
Jim's *clothing. As* Jim *draws back half afraid*)
There—there, now, don't you be afraid of Ben
Gunn—

Jim. I'm not afraid.

Gunn. That's right—I've lived that rough you'd
be ashamed to hear—just look at these—(*indicates
his clothing*) Rags! Tatters! Pieces of old
ship's canvas and bits of old sea cloth—All held
together with brass buttons and bits of stick and
loops of tarry gaskin—Now—you look at me—
you'd never think I had a pious mother. Would
you, now?

Jim. Why—no—not particularly.

Gunn. Ah, well, I had—remarkable pious.
And I was a civil pious boy and could rattle off my
catechism that fast as you couldn't tell one word
from another—fact—and here's what it came to,
Jim. (*Points about the island*) And it began with
chuck-fathen in a cemetery on the blessed graves-
stones. That's what it begun with, but it went
farther'n that; and so my mother told me and
predicted the whole, she did, the pious woman.

Jim. But how did you get here?

Gunn. It were Providence that put me here.
I've thought it all out on this here lonely island
and I'm back on piety. You don't catch me tasting
rum so much but just a thimble-full for luck, .of
course, the first chance I get—I'm bound I'll be

good and—(*Takes him by the arm*) I see the way to. (*Confidentially and looking about*) And, Jim—I'm rich.

JIM. (*Starting and trying to draw away*) Rich—you—why——

GUNN. Rich! Rich! I says——

JIM. But——

GUNN. And I'll tell you what; I'll make a man of you, Jim. You'll bless your stars, you will; you was the first that found me and—(*Suddenly with great change and intensity*) Now, Jim, you tell me true——

JIM. Tell you what?

GUNN. That ain't Flint's ship out there! It ain't!

JIM. No. And Flint is dead.

GUNN. (*With evident relief*) Ah——

JIM. But I'll tell you true as you ask me; there are some of Flint's hands aboard—worse luck for the rest of us.

GUNN. (*Eagerly*) Not a man—with one—leg?

JIM. Silver?

GUNN. Aye—Silver——

JIM. He's cook and ring-leader, too.

GUNN. (*Anxiously*) If you was sent by Long John I'm as good as pork and I know it——

JIM. I'm not sent by Silver.

GUNN. Now, tell me true, Jim—you tell me true——

JIM. I'm running from him—He and his hands mutinied on us——

GUNN. On who, mate?

JIM. Squire Trelawney—and Captain Smollett and Dr. Livesey——

GUNN. Mutinied, you say, Jim?

JIM. Yes. We had come on that ship to look for Flint's treasure.

GUNN. (*Startled*) Eh? (*Crosses to cave*)

JIM. We had Flint's map——

GUNN. Flint's fist! And where did you get that? (*Crosses to* JIM C.)

JIM. I got it—from Bill Bones—when he died.

GUNN. Billy Bones dead, too!

JIM. I gave it to the squire. Somehow, Silver got wind of it—he managed to deceive the Squire by appearing kindly and——

GUNN. Aye, that would be Silver's way—There was Flint—Barring rum, his match was never seen. He were afraid of none—not he; on'y Silver— Silver was that genteel——

JIM. Well, last night they made a demand for the map. The Squire was in a hard way and gave it to them——

GUNN. Flint's fist?

JIM. No, a false map.

GUNN. Oho! Not the right one.

JIM. No, but I think Silver suspected—he made me come along with them—as soon as the boats grounded, I jumped—then I ran with all my might through the woods. All night, I wandered about— until I found you. And now, sir, since I've told you, won't you help me get back to my friends? Won't you, please?

GUNN. (*Knowingly*) So, your Squire gave 'em a false map and kept the real one? (*Sits on rock*)

JIM. Yes.

GUNN. That's a good 'un.

(*As* GUNN *starts to laugh.*)

JIM. What—what is it?

GUNN. You're all in a clove hitch, ain't you? All in a clove hitch!

JIM. You will help me, won't you?

GUNN. (*Growing serious*) You just put your trust in Ben Gunn. Ben Gunn's the man to do it.

JIM. Then you'll send me back—(GUNN *beckons* JIM, JIM *sits* R. *of* GUNN)

GUNN. Would you think it likely now your Squire would prove liberally minded in case of help —him being in a clove hitch.

JIM. Oh, I'm sure he would.

GUNN. Aye, but you see I didn't mean giving me a gate to keep and a suit of livery clothes and such; that's not my Mark, Jim—(*As* JIM *starts to reply*) What I mean is would he likely come down to the toon of, say, one thousand pounds out of money that's as good as a man's own already?

JIM. You can count on it—all the hands were to share——

GUNN. And a passage home? And a passage home?

JIM. The Squire's a gentleman——

GUNN. A gentleman born, not a gentleman of fortune, eh, Jim?

JIM. Of course. Besides, if we get rid of the others, we should want you to help work the vessel home——

GUNN. Aye, so you would. (*Crosses down* L.)

JIM. And now, will you tell me how to get back to my friends—will you?

GUNN. So much I'll tell you, and no more——

JIM. Yes?

GUNN. I were in Flint's ship when he buried the treasure.

JIM. You!

GUNN. He and six along—six strong seamen. They was ashore nigh on a week and us waitin' in the bay in the old Walrus. One day up went the signal and here come Flint, his head done up in a blue scarf—in a little boat—and all by himself.

JIM. By himself—but the others?

GUNN. The sun was up and mortal white he looked about the cutwater. But there he was, you mind, and the six all dead—dead and buried. How he done it, not a man aboard us could make out.

It was battle, murder, and sudden death—him against six.

JIM. He killed them all?

GUNN. Aye—Billy Bones was mate; Long John, he was quartermaster; and they asked him where the treasure was—" Ah," says he " You can go ashore if you like and stay. But as for the ship, she'll beat up for more, by thunder." That's what he said.

JIM. But then—how—how did you come here?

BUNN. I was in another ship three years back and we sighted this island; " Boys " said I," here's Flint's treasure; let's land and find it." The Cap'n was displeased at that but my messmates were all of one mind. Twelve days they looked for it and every day they had a worse word for me until one fine morning all hands went aboard. " As for you, Benjamin Gunn," says they, " here's a musket," they says, " and a spade and pickaxe. You stay here and find Flint's money for yourself," they says.

JIM. Marooned you!

GUNN. Well, Jim, three years I've been here and not a bite of Christian diet from that day to this. But now, look here—look at me——

JIM. Well?

GUNN. Do I look like a man before the mast? Do I?

JIM. No.

GUNN. No, says you—Nor I weren't neither, says I.

JIM. But then——

GUNN. Just you mention them words to your Squire—nor he weren't neither—that's the word.

JIM. But I don't understand.

GUNN. (*With more and more significance*) Three years I were the man of this island; light and dark, fair and rain, and sometimes I would, maybe, think upon a prayer, says you—and sometimes I would, maybe, think of my old mother, so be as she's alive. You'll say—but the most part of Gunn's time—this is what you'll say—the most part of his time was took up with another matter—and then you'll give him a nip—like I do——(*Pinches* JIM *in the ribs*)

JIM. What do you mean?

GUNN. Then you'll up and you'll say this: Gunn's a good man—you'll say and he puts a precious sight more confidence—a precious sight mind you—in a gen'lman born than in these gen'lmen of fortune—having been one himself. (*Spits*)

JIM. I don't understand a word you're saying-but how on earth am I to tell these things to the Squire—if I can't get aboard?

GUNN. Ah, there's the hitch for sure.

JIM. Can't you help me someway—can't you?

GUNN. Aye, lad—you put your trust in Ben Gunn.

JIM. (*Eagerly*) Then, will you? Will you help m?

GUNN. Aye—(*Crosses to boat* R. C. *up. Points to his boat*) There's my boat—I made it with my two hands.

JIM. You'll let me take it?

GUNN. Aye, lad. You may take it——

JIM. And you'll come, too. You'll help me reach the boat?

GUNN. Nay, lad—not Ben Gunn—but you can have the coracle——

JIM. Then, I'll go alone—Here, help me launch it. (*As he starts to push out the boat, there is heard a salvo of shots*) What—what was that? (*Crosses to Rock* C.)

GUNN. Shots!

JIM. Then they've begun the fight already—what shall I do now?

GUNN. Wait. (*Crawls up the side of rock and*

peers anxiously in the distance) That wasn't from the boat——

JIM. Where then?

GUNN. (*Up on rock*) Wait! (*Suddenly he utters a cry*)

JIM. What is it?

GUNN. (*Excitedly. Looks off* R.) Look—look —there—what do you see?

JIM. The Union Jack.

GUNN. Aye, lad, the Union Jack, flying over the old stockade as was made years and years ago by Flint—there are your friends, Jim.

JIM. More like the mutineers.

GUNN. No, Silver would fly the Jolly Roger, you don't make no doubt of that. No, that's your friends. There's been blows and I reckon your friend has had the best of it.

JIM. Then come—come—quick. (*Down from rock to* C.)

GUNN. (*Follows, holding* JIM *back*) Nay, mate, Ben Gunn is fly. Rum wouldn't bring me there where you're going—not rum wouldn't, till I see your born gen'lman and gets it on his word of honor.

JIM. Then let me go.

GUNN. (*Still holding* JIM) You won't forget my words——

JIM. No—no——

GUNN. "A precious sight—that's what you'll say—a precious sight more confidence" and then nips him, eh?

JIM. (*Always trying to get away*) Yes—yes

GUNN. And when Ben Gunn's wanted you know where to find him, Jim?

JIM. No—where?

GUNN. Just where you found him to-day; and him that comes is to have a white thing in his hand and he's to come alone—you—understand? eh?

Jim. Yes. I think so—you have something to propose and you wish to see the Squire or the Doctor—here—is that it?

Gunn. And when, says you—Why, from noon observation to about six bells.

Jim. Good. Now may I go?

Gunn. You won't forget?

Jim. No—no——

Gunn. Precious sight and reasons of his own, says you. Reasons of his own—that's the main-stay.

Jim. Yes—yes—now, please—please——

Gunn. And, Jim, if you was to see Silver you wouldn't go to sell Ben Gunn? Wild horses wouldn't draw it from you?

Jim. No—no—I swear it.

Gunn. Well, then, I reckon you can go—(*Lets him go and* Jim *darts away.* Gunn *calls after him*) Remember " precious sight—and reasons of his own " (*Turns to his own cave*) If them pirates camp ashore—there'll be widders in the morning.

CURTAIN.

ACT III.

Scene 2:—*The Stockade. Upon three sides, wherever visible, high walls, of rude planks, spike-shaped at top. At Center and Back the front of a log-house, with porch and door. Back of house tall, large trees. At* L. 2 *a wooden gate with wooden bar to fasten it. At several places about the walls, peek-holes and gun-rests. At center of stage, a sawed-off log which serves as a table, with other smaller logs which are used as seats. The floor is covered with sand. When Curtain goes up,* Gray,

Hunter, Redruth, Joyce are stationed at different sides each with gun to his shoulder, and each peering through a peek-hole. On the table in the center, stands Captain Smollett, an old-fashioned spy-glass to his eye. Beside him stand Dr. Livesey and the Squire. Before the curtain rises there is heard the report of a cannon, fired at intervals. When the curtain rises reports continue.

Smollett. Blaze away—blaze away. That's right—you've little enough powder left.

Squire. (*Draws Dr. Livesey aside*) We're beaten, doctor. They have us here like rats in a trap.

Dr. Livesey. And Hawkins—the lad was like one of my own.

Squire. They've got us. We've got to give in—Captain Smollett—we're come to the end.

Smollett. (*Drops glass, surprised*) What's that.

Squire. I am responsible for these men here—I can't see them murdered—I'm willing to do anything.

Smollett. Well, I'm not—and I don't think these men are, either.

Squire. What's that?

Smollett. (*Crosses L.*) My lads, you heard what the Squire said—now then, what do you say—Shall we give up or stand here and fight like Englishmen——

Omnes. Fight! To the end, sir.

Smollett. (*To Squire*) You see I knew I could count on 'em—and now I tell you—we're not beaten yet—There's still a chance—For the last half hour I've looked at that ship—and only two have I seen aboard her.

Squire. Well.

Smollett. As soon as it grows dark, one or two

of us will creep down to the beach, row out and cut that ship adrift.

Dr. Livesey. Yes, but how about the rest of that crew of pirates—not a sound have we heard from them the last hour.

Smollett. That's what I mean to find out. I must know at once where the enemy is—and what he is planning—In short I need volunteers to reconnoiter.

(Gray *and* Hunter *step up at once.*)

Gray. We'll go, sir.

Squire. Wait—Before you offer I want you to know the risk—It's life or death.

Hunter. We're ready, sir.

Smollett. Keep to the left and under cover as much as possible—try for the woods.

Gray. Right, sir.

Smollett. (*To* Joyce *at peek-hole*) All clear, Joyce?

Joyce. Yes, sir.

Smollett. Off with you, then——

Squire. (*Standing in front of gate*) If you men succeed, we'll owe you our lives—I'll remember it.

Smollett. (*Standing in front of gate.* Hunter *and* Gray *exit*) Careful, now—I tell you if we can do this we'll turn a trick on them——

(*Another cannon shot booms out.*)

Squire. Captain, it seems to me it's our flag they're aiming at—Wouldn't it be wiser tó take it in?

Smollett. Strike my colors! No, sir, not I!

Squire. We shall have to do it sooner or later— we're outnumbered three to one—beaten in every way. I'm willing to give them that chart if they'll return young Hawkins to us and let us go.

Dr. Livesey. And I, Captain Smollett. I'd see the whole treasure in Davy Jones' locker rather than any harm should come to Jiu

(*Several pistol shots ring out. There is a cry and a call.*)

Joyce. (*Excitedly*) Hunter and Gray, sir.
Smollett. What?
Squire. (*Who has rushed up excitedly*) Hunter's wounded.
Smollett. The gates—quick. (*They open the gates. Exclamations ad lib.* Hunter *supported by* Gray *enters.* Hunter *is badly wounded. The* Doctor *immediately rushes to him.* Smollett *speaks to* Gray) Well? Well?
Gray. They're all in the woods there—on every side—I got one of 'em I think.
Smollett. In your places. (*The* Doctor Livesey *who is bending over* Hunter) Is he badly hurt, Dr. Livesey?
Dr. Livesey. Yes—very.
Hunter. (*As he takes the water*) Be I going, doctor?
Dr. Livesey. Tom—my man—you're going home.
Hunter. I wish I had had a lick at 'em first.
Squire. (*Bends over* Tom) Tom—Tom——
Hunter. Yes, sir?
Squire. Say you forgive me, Tom—for bringing you along.
Hunter. Would that be respectful, sir?
Squire. Aye—do Tom.
Hunter. Alright. Howso ever it be—so be it—amen. (*Falls back*)
Dr. Livesey. Here, Gray—give me a hand— we'll carry him in.

(Gray *and* Dr. Livesey *carry in* Hunter.)

SQUIRE. And it's my fault—all my fault for bringing him.

SMOLLETT. No time for that now, sir. Those men out there are planning an attack—that's it— waiting to creep up in the dusk.

SQUIRE. All the better for us——

SMOLLETT. If we win—yes—if not—(GRAY *and* DR. LIVESEY *return. To* DR. LIVESEY) Well?

DR. LIVESEY. He's gone, sir.

SQUIRE. Poor lad—poor lad——

DR. LIVESEY. Aye—and how about the lad out there—with them.

SMOLLETT. We'll know that very soon or I miss my guess.

SILVER. Ahoy!

SMOLLETT. Those blackguards out there will not catch us unprepared; we're ready for them when they come.

SILVER. Ahoy!

SMOLLETT. What's that? Listen!

VOICE. (*Without*) Log-house, ahoy! Log-house, ahoy!

(*They all rush to the peek-holes and peer out.*)

SMOLLETT. Silver as I live.

DR. LIVESEY. With a flag of true.

SQUIRE. What do you suppose——

SMOLLETT. Some trick—they know we've dis-covered their presence—(*Then turns to men*) All stand ready and watch—(*The men take their places about the stockade and peer out through the peek-holes*) Gray, stand by those gates. (GRAY *takes his place at the gates*) Wait till I give the word.

SILVER. (*Without*) Ahoy! Log-house ahoy!

SMOLLETT. Who goes? Stand or we fire!

SILVER. (*Without*) Flag of truce!

SMOLLETT. (*Calls to* SILVER) What do you want with your flag of truce?

SILVER. (*Without*) Captain Silver, come aboard to make terms.

SQUIRE. What?

SMOLLETT. Easy! (*To* SQUIRE) It's a trick I tell you—(*To* SILVER) You come alone?

SILVER. (*Without*) Alone.

DR. LIVESEY. (*Low to* SMOLLETT *as* GRAY *opens the gates*) Find out about Hawkins—if you can. Agree to anything—make any terms so you get the boy——

(SMOLLETT *turns as* SILVER *enters.*)

SILVER. (*As gates close behind him*) Flag of truce—you respect a flag of truce?

SMOLLETT. (*Severely*) If there's any treachery, Silver—it will be on your side—and the Lord help you!

SILVER. That's enough, Captain—a word from you's enough. (*Looks about*) Ah, Squire, the top of the morning to you—Doctor, here's my service.

SMOLLETT. (*Severely*) If you have anything to say—better say it!

SILVER. Right you are, Cap'n Smollett—Well, then we're willing to submit if we can come to terms and no bones about it.

SQUIRE. (*Eagerly and joyfully*) What, you——

SMOLLETT. (*To* SQUIRE) Wait—(*To* SILVER) What terms?

SILVER. That was a good lay of yours sending us on that wild-goose chase, with that false chart. It was a clever trick—to get us out of the way, while you reached here—only——

SMOLLETT. Well!

SILVER. It won't work twice—I suspected you even then—that's why I took Hawkins. But now, here you are—and there's your ship with the Jolly Roger flying at her mast-head—you lost most of your provisions coming here and I know just about how much ammunition you got——

SMOLLETT. That's our affair.

SILVER. And ours—(*With sudden fierceness*) We've got you, I tell you, and you've got to do what I say—We want that treasure and we want it now. That's our point.

SMOLLETT. Point enough.

SILVER. You want your lives and that's your point. Now, you give us that chart and then either you come aboard along with us, once the treasure is shipped, and then I'll give you my affy-davy, upon my word of honor, to clap you somewhere safe ashore.

SMOLLETT. (*Sarcastically*) Of course we can trust you to do that?

SILVER. Well, then, if that ain't to your fancy, some of my hands being rough, you can stay here and we'll divide stores with you, and I give you my affy-davy, as before, to speak the first ship we sight and send 'em here to pick you up. Now, you'll own that's talking. (*Turns round to the men*) I hope all hands will overhaul my words, for what is spoke to one is spoke to all.

SMOLLETT. And is that all?

SILVER. Every last word, by thunder. Refuse and you've seen the last of me but musket-balls.

SMOLLETT. (*Crosses to* L.) Then hear me, if you'll come one by one—I'll engage to clap you all in irons.

SILVER. Oh——

SMOLLETT. And take you home for trial.

SILVER. You will—will you?

SMOLLETT. You can't find that treasure without us—you can't work that ship without us——

SILVER. Look out, I warn you!

SMOLLETT. You need us more than we need you——

SILVER. Oh, we do, do we? You wouldn't stand there and defy me if we still had that boy. If

Hawkins hadn't got away I'd have you on your knees fast enough.

DR. LIVESEY. Hawkins safe? Thank God!

SMOLLETT. Now bundle out of this, double quick. I'll put a bullet in your back when next me meet.

SILVER. That's your last word?

SMOLLETT. It is.

SILVER. Alright, my men are waiting for me to give the word. You'll hear from me in the next five minutes—I'll stave your old blockhouse in like a rum puncheon—(SMOLLETT *laughs derisively*) Laugh, by thunder, laugh—before a quarter of an hour's out, you'll laugh on the other side. (*Turns and looks at the men*) And them that die'll be the lucky ones. (*Stalks out,* GRAY *closes the door behind him*)

SMOLLETT. (*Turns to men*) Now lads, I've given Silver a broadside—pitched it in red hot on purpose and before many minutes are out, as he said, we'll be boarded. We're outnumbered but we fight in shelter and I believe we can drub 'em— That's why I put it on so thick—to make 'em fight —We can stand anything but what he threatened— a siege or being marooned—so let them come, lads— let them come. (*They all turn to get ready most of them taking off their coats*) Doctor, you take the rear there.

DR. LIVESEY. (*As he goes to his position in the back*) Aye, aye, sir——

SMOLLETT. Joyce, the south side. (JOYCE *takes his position*) Mr. Trelawney. You and Gray will take the North. (JOYCE *fires*) What—what was that?

JOYCE. Thought I saw something——

SMOLLETT. (*Comes up and looks over* JOYCE'S *shoulder*) Hit him?

JOYCE. Don't know, sir.

SMOLLETT. Wait—easy now—(*Peers out intently*)

Joyce. There—in the trees to the right—Don't you see something moving——

Smollett. Yes—wait—he's coming nearer—get ready—now, wait till he gets to the open, now then, ready and—(*Suddenly stumbles back*) Oh, my God!—it's Jim!

Dr. Livesey. (*Comes rushing up*) What?

Smollett. Don't call. See—to the left—they're watching—now ready, Joyce—shout to the left when I call—ready?

Joyce. Ready.

Smollett. On the gate, Doctor. (*The* Doctor *goes to the gate and unbars it*) Now then—(*Calls*) Jim! Come—come now—come, lad! (*To* Joyce) Shoot—shoot man! (Joyce *shoots. There is a rattle of musketry from the outside and then a slight pause*) My God—did they get him—did they?

(Jim *comes rushing in. The* Doctor *grabs him in his arms.*)

Dr. Livesey. Thank God you're safe, lad.

Jim. They almost got me, sir——

Squire. Where have you been?

Dr. Livesey. How did you escape?

Jim. I'll explain all that later, sir—there's something else you ought to know—I've met a man who has been here on this island three years. Ben Gunn he says his name is; he seems to have something to propose.

Squire. A man on the island?

Gray. I see something moving, sir——

Smollett. Back to your places. (Doctor *and* Squire *go to their places*) Jim, you go into the house—get under cover——

Jim. No, sir, I'll stay here and help you, sir.

Joyce. I think I see them over here too, sir.

Dr. Livesey. Aye, and here, too——

Gray. And here, sir——

Smollett.   Then it's from all sides—they're getting ready for a charge—Now hold steady.

Squire.   They're starting——

Smollett.   Save your ammunition until they reach open——

Dr. Livesey.   Here they come.

Smollett.   Then let them have it.

(*There are cries and shouts together with shots from the outside. Those within the stockade return the fire, while* Jim *and* Smollett *are busy loading and relaying muskets.*)

Squire.   I got one of them.

Gray.   And I, sir——

Dr. Livesey.   Four of them—on this side—they're making for the wall.

Smollett.   Shoot—Keep 'em away. Don't let 'em over—at 'em lads. (*The sounds have increased. Cries, curses and musket shots are heard*) Look out there—you Redruth—over your head—(*Above another pirate's head, there appears a pirate with a red kerchief over his head and a knife in his mouth over Man's head. Man shoots and the pirate falls*) That's it. (*Three pirates led by* Anderson *break over the wall. The fight now is a running one both within and without the stockade*) You—Squire—Gray—back into the house, lads—we'll fight them there.

(*One pirate rushes at* Redruth—*and stuns in fight. Another rushes at the* Doctor *and forces him to flee. The fight is going very much with the pirates. It is now a running fight about the house, with cutlasses and pistols. For a time it is heard rather than seen for it is behind the house and within it. Then suddenly from one side of the house there comes running,* Anderson, *cutlass in hand.*)

ANDERSON. (*Rushing forward*) Oh, men—don't leave one of 'em—not a one—(*Suddenly* JIM *comes rushing from the side opposite* ANDERSON *and runs full tilt into him and is caught*) So, it's you—you young rascal—well, here's where we settles with you.

JIM. Oh, let me go—let me go——

ANDERSON. Let you go—aye—here's where you go a long, long ways, lad. (*He raises his cutlass.* JIM *shrieks. Then suddenly there is a pistol shot and* ANDERSON *falls.* GRAY *comes running around the corner*)

GRAY. I was just in time, lad.

(*From the back of the house and inside there come running the pirates pursued by the* DOCTOR, SQUIRE *and* SMOLLETT. *The pirates make for the wall.*)

SMOLLETT. After them—don't let them get away —don't let 'em escape——

(*Suddenly one of the pirates upon the top of the stockade turns and fires deliberately at* SMOLLETT *and* SMOLLETT *stumbles back and finally falls.*)

DR. LIVESEY. Captain—you're wounded.

SMOLLETT. Now, listen—quick—Before they can reach the beach—Beat 'em to the Hispaniola and cut her adrift. The tide will carry her to the North inlet. Once there and you've got 'em, I tell you— you've got 'em. Go—go—quick—save the ship.

JIM. I'll go——

DR. LIVESEY. No—no, Jim.

JIM. The Captain said to save the ship and I am going to do it

CURTAIN.

ACT III.

SCENE: 3:—*The Hispaniola tossing at sea. The ship is in motion but evidently not under control. She is under her mainsail and two jibs. The sails droop at times and then fill with the report of a gun. The tiller spins round from side to side. The boat tosses and pitches as the sea runs high. Two men, BLACK DOG and HANDS, are seen upon the deck of the ship " locked together in deadly wrestle, each with a hand upon the other's throat." Finally they separate for a moment and then knives flash. BLACK DOG, by a quick movement, wounds HANDS in the leg. As he starts to follow up his advantage, HANDS turns quickly, catches BLACK DOG by the neck and holds him back against the rigging, his knife at his throat. Both are drunk.*

HANDS. (*As he gets his wound*) Oh—you—would—you would—would you—Now, then—(*The boat lurches. At the same instant HANDS makes a lunge and catches BLACK DOG*) Now then—speak—you set the ship adrift—you did! Say it! Say it!

O'BRIEN. (*Struggling*) No—no——

HANDS. You'll never tell that to Silver—Now for the last time, say it. Say it, or——

O'BRIEN. No!

HANDS. Then there. (*Stabs him*) You'll never tell Silver—(*Shakes him again and again as he speaks*) Ugh! (*Throws him from him. Tries to stumble over the deck, but is forced to catch the rigging of the mainsail*) What's this—by thunder he got me—he got me—I can't see—what is it? (*Growing more and more terrified*) I've gone blind—I've gone blind. (*Sinks back in the rigging, trying to hold himself up, apparently in a faint. For a moment there is silence while the boat tosses from side to side.* JIM *appears climbing over the side of the boat. For a moment he looks about, timidly and afraid. Then he calls*)

JIM. Ahoy! Ship-mates, ahoy! (*He waits for an answer. When he gets none he scrambles down on deck and with pistols drawn goes carefully over the boat. Finally he sees* O'BRIEN *dead and* HANDS *apparently dead. He starts back*) Oh! Dead! (*As he starts away there is a groan.* JIM *turns quickly. He is very frightened. With a cry he rushes out and on the companionway. He comes back almost at once*) Gone! All gone! I've got the ship—I've got the ship. (*He turns to go to the tiller*) If I can only sail her—(*As he hears a groan*) Who's that? (*He waits for an answer. When he gets none he stands fearfully waiting. Again a groan*) Answer—answer, or I fire!

HANDS. (*Moans feebly*) It's Israel Hands, lad.

JIM. So, it's you, Mr. Hands. Huch hurt?

HANDS. I'm dying—dying—I can't move——

JIM. See that you don't—for at the first move I shoot——

HANDS. And where mought you have come from?

JIM. I've come to take possession of this ship. (*As* HANDS *laughs*) So, Mr. Hands, you'll regard me as Captain until further notice.

HANDS. (*Wickedly*) Cap'n, eh?

JIM. (*Presenting his pistols*) Is it understood, Mr. Hands?

HANDS. Aye—it's understood——

JIM. Then first we'll strike those colors—(*Pulls down the Jolly Roger*) There, God save the king and there's an end to Captain Silver, too. (*Throws flag overboard*)

HANDS. Will you tell me how you mought have come aboard?

JIM. All night I've been below in a little boat— It was I who cut the ship adrift.

HANDS. You. And I killed him there for it. I'm going to——

JIM. You've been drifting all night. I'm going to beach this ship—at the North inlet—where we can get off the provisions—and where Silver will never find her——

HANDS. All alone, eh?

JIM. Yes, alone.

HANDS. Ever sail a boat, mate?

JIM. I'm going to sail this one—(*Sinister*) with your help, Mr. Hands——

HANDS. Oho—with my help, is it?

JIM. Just so, Mr. Hands.

HANDS. Now, I'll make a bargain with you, Hawkins.

JIM. Captain Hawkins!

HANDS. Captain Hawkins—this leg's bleeding— I'll die—I will—if you don't give me a hand. Give me a kerchief to tie my wound up and some food and drink—and I'll tell you how to sail her—and that's about square.

JIM. (*Suspiciously*) You know where the North Inlet is?

HANDS. To be sure——

JIM. You'll take her there?

HANDS. Aye.

JIM. Mind, at the first sign of any treachery from you——

HANDS. I'm no such fool. Go below and get me some brandy.

JIM. No——

HANDS. But you said——

Jim. First the boat——

Hands. Smart lad—take no chances—well, have it your way—take a haul on the mainsail there—(Jim *goes to the mainsail and pulls at the ropes to make her fast*) Hold her tight—there. (*As* Jim *works,* Hands *seems always to be growing stronger and wilier*) She'll sail under the mainsail alone. Now put your helm hard alee—(Hands *becomes more and more active while* Jim's *eyes are upon steering, he surreptitiously tries and is able to move back and forth*) It's a narrow channel—you'll have to feel your way.

Jim. She's safe so far——

Hands. You're doing fine, lad—couldn't do better myself—and now—come here.

Jim. (*Comes up*) What do you want?

Hands. A little drop of brandy. I've earned it now.

Jim. Alright—I'll get it—You're sure the boat will be alright?

Hands. She'll hold steady.

Jim. Alright. (Jim *enters cabin,* Hands *crawls to knife, hides it in his bosom and returns to former position as* Jim *returns*) I couldn't find any —not a drop left.

Hands. Jim, I'm for my long home, lad, this time—and no mistake. Come here.

(*As* Jim *comes a step nearer* Hands *places his hand in his jacket where he has concealed the knife.*)

Jim. (*Startled, draws his pistols*) None of that —take your hand out—take it out or—I'll——

Hands. (*Draw out his hand with stick of tobacco*) Just getting my tobacco—see—will you cut me a junk of that—I haven't any knife.

Jim. (*Hesitates*) Throw it here. (Hands *throws him the tobacco and he starts to cut it*) If

I were in your place I'd be thinking of prayers and
not tobacco——

HANDS. Why? Tell me that?

JIM. Why—You've broken your trust—you've
lived in sin and lies and blood—and you ask me
why? For God's mercy—that's why, Mr. Hands.
(JIM *gives him back the tobacco and goes to the
tiller*) I can see the beach from here——

HANDS. Haul that mailsail a notch—All right
lad——

JIM. All right sir——

(HANDS *now, knife in hand, has worked up back
of* JIM. JIM, *holding the tiller, has not noticed
him; but the moment that* HANDS *throws himself forward with a cry,* JIM *suddenly sees him
and throws himself aside to avoid the blow.
As he does so, he lets go the tiller which springs
back and hits* HANDS *across the chest, stopping
him. "Before he could recover I was safe out
of the corner where he had trapped me, with
all the deck to dodge about. Just forward of
the mainmast I stopped, drew from my pocket
my pistol, though he was once more coming
directly toward me.")*

Stop—stop—or I fire.

HANDS. You little rat—I've got a score to settle
with you. (*Starts forward*) Stop! (*As* HANDS
still comes forward)

JIM. Stop! (*As* HANDS *still comes forward*)
Stop! Well then, take it. (*He pulls the trigger,
the gun doesn't explode*)

HANDS. (*With a cry of exultation*) Aha, so the
guns don't go off—never thought to prime 'em, my
fine Captain—Now then, my brave lad—you're going
to save the boat, are you—we'll see—we'll see—

(*Meanwhile* HANDS *had been approaching and* JIM
has been fleeing. "Wounded as he was it was

wonderful how fast he was. I had no time to try my other pistol. One thing I saw I must simply retreat before me or he would speedily hold me boxed in the stern. I placed my hands on the mainmast and waited, every nerve stretched. Seeing I meant to dodge he also paused and a moment or two passed in feints on his part and correspondent movements on mine. It was such a game as I had often played at home about the rocks. And I thought I could hold my own at it against an elderly seaman with a wounded thigh. Well, while I stood thus, suddenly the Hispanolia struck, staggered, ground for an instant on the sand and then swift as a blow canted over on the port side till the deck stood at an angle of about forty-five degrees. We were both capsized in a second and both of us rolled about together into the scuppers, but I was first to foot again. The sudden canting of the ship made the deck no place for running and I had to find some new way of escape, quick as thought I sprang into the mizzen shrouds, rattled up hand over hand and did not draw breath until I was safe on the cross trees.")

(*As they play a sort of grim hide and seek he makes a movement and misses* JIM) By thunder if this leg were right—it would be quick work for you—but I'll get you—you'll not get out of this corner—I've got you now—I've got you——

(*As* HANDS *almost corners* JIM, *the boat strikes and they are tumbled together.* JIM *scurries to the mainmast.*)

JIM. Not yet—Mr. Hands—not yet. (*Scurries up the mainmast*)
HANDS. If that boat hadn't struck—I'd have had

you—and I've got you now. You can't get down—
I'v got you up a tree my fine Captain.

JIM. (*Draws other pistol*)   I still have another
pistol, Mr. Hands.   It is not like the other—This
one is primed.   Another step and I'll blow your
brains out——

HANDS. (*Stops*) Eh?

JIM. Drop that knife, Mr. Hands—drop that
knife—drop it I say.

HANDS. Drop it—very well lad—(*Suddenly hurls
the dagger*) There, take it.

JIM. (*With a cry as the knife strikes him in the
shoulder, turns away*) Oh! (*Then as* HANDS *with
shout makes toward him, he pulls the triggers on
the pistols and* HANDS, *with a cry, pitches forward
as* JIM *lets fall the pistols. With an effort,* JIM,
*crying out under the pain finally wrenches his
shoulder free and then tottering and almost faint he
cries*) The stockade! Now for the stockade!

CURTAIN.

ACT IV.

SCENE I :—*The Stockade. When the curtain rises
it is early dawn. The pirates are in possession
of the stockade, but there are only six of them
left. These are asleep about the stockade.*
SILVER *leans against one of the posts of the
porch, asleep, his parrot perched upon a stick
just above him. Among the pirates are* MERRY,
MORGAN, DIRK *and* ANDERSON. *Several of
them have their heads bandaged as if wounded.*

*For a moment after the curtain goes up noth-
ing happens. Then over the wall there comes*
JIM. *In the half light he stumbles around, peering at the sleepers. Finally he comes up to*

SILVER and then he discovers that the pirates now occupy the stockade. With a cry, he stumbles back and starts away, but just as he does so the parrot cries out—" Pieces of eight," " Pieces of eight." Immediately there is a stir and JIM as he runs toward the gate bolts into MERRY who has awakened and is sitting up on the ground.

JIM. Squire—Squire—Silver!
MERRY. (*Catching* JIM *who struggles*) No, you don't—No, you don't——
JIM. Let me be; let me be——
MERRY. Silver!—Silver!
SILVER. (*They are all awake by this time and it is now light*) What is it?
MERRY. Look here. Here's a nice little catch—
SILVER. (*Comes up*) Well, shiver my timbers, if it ain't Jim Hawkins.
MERRY. Aye, and looking as brash as ever.
MORGAN. I'd like to——
SILVER. (*Forestalling* MORGAN) Come, lad, speak up—(*As* JIM *stands with his back against the wall and refuses to answer*) Just dropped in for an early morning call? (*Still* JIM *refuses to answer*) Now, I take that friendly—well, lad,—speak up—speak up.
JIM. Dr. Livesey and Squire Trelawney——
SILVER. This here gets me—it do—but lad, I'm going to know what you been up to.
JIM. I'll not say a word till you tell me where my friends are.
MORGAN. What!
MERRY. The little rat! (*Both he and* MORGAN *make a movement toward* JIM)
SILVER. (*To* MORGAN *and* MERRY) Who's cap'n here? (*Turning to* JIM) I want you to recognize your position—here you are with us, who, you'll admit ain't got no cause to be too friendly.

Dirk. Aye, that's right.

Silver. So the truth, lad—the truth——

Jim. I have a right to know first—what's what—why you're here and where my friends are.

Merry. Wot's wot! Ah, he'd be a lucky one as knowed that!

Silver. (*To* Merry) Batten down your hatches. (*To* Jim) Now, come, lad—come——

Jim. Not until you tell me——

Morgan. You won't, eh—we'll see——

Silver. (*To* Morgan) Hold there, Tom Morgan. (*As* Morgan *growls angrily*) Jim's right—it's only fair he knows. (*Turns to* Jim) Last night, down came Dr. Livesey with a flag of truce. " Silver " says he, " let's bargain——

Merry. (*Derisively*) A pretty bargain it was—

Silver. (*Angrily to* Merry) It's the bargain I made—him and me—him and his friends to give up this place—and us not to touch 'em——

Morgan. And why?

Silver. Because they had ammunition we needed—because they had this place we needed—because they can't get away ——

Jim. Why did they change then?

Silver. They thought—they'd get out and make for the ship and leave us here—and I let 'em think so—(*Sinisterly*) I've got the only boat to reach that ship—and I've got it hidden—I've beaten them—fooled them at every turn——

Jim. Oh, have you?

Silver. Aye, by gum, I have——

Jim. Well then, look there. The ship's gone!

Silver. Well, shiver my timbers!

(*There is great astonishment among the men. For a moment they seem stunned. Then suddenly there is growing excitement.*)

Morgan. Marooned.

MERRY. Tricked—beaten—fooled—(*With a sudden cry they make a dash toward* JIM)

SILVER. Wait! (*As the men growl angrily* SILVER *speaks meaningly to* JIM)

JIM. (*At bay*) I'm not such a fool that I don't know what I have to look for—(*The men shout at him. "Aye—aye—" and threaten*) Well, let the worst come—it's little I care—but there's a thing or two I have to tell you first—You're in a bad way—ship's lost—treasure's lost—men lost—your whole business gone to wreck. (*There is a growl from the man*) And do you want to know who did it? Why I did it.

MORGAN. (*Starts for* JIM) You——

MERRY. I'll slit his throat—I'll——

(SILVER *thunders at* MERRY *and* MORGAN.)

JIM. I was in the apple barrel—I heard you anɩ Morgan and Hands, all of you—and told every word of it. And as for the Hispaniola—it was I who cut her hawser—It was I who killed the men you had aboard her.

SILVER. You—You——

JIM. I killed them I tell you and I brought that ship where you'll never se her more, not one of you. The laugh's on my side. I've had the top of this business from the first and I no more fear you than I do a fly! (*As the men threaten but are held back by* SILVER) Kill me if you please or spare me—but one thing I'll say—if you spare me, bygones are bygones, and when you fellows are in court for piracy—I'll save you all I can—Kill me and do yourselves no good or spare me and keep a witness to save you from the gallows.

(*The men with the exception of* SILVER *are in a little group whispering together.* SILVER *stands and stares at* JIM.)

SILVER. (*His manner has changed. He is no*

*longer threatening, but rather sly as if feeling his
way)* So, you cut the boat adrift?

JIM.   Yes.

SILVER.   And you know where it is, eh?

JIM.   But I'm not going to tell.

ARROW.   That boy's not going to live.

MORGAN.   Then by thunder here goes. *(MORGAN
with knife drawn springs toward JIM R. C., but
SILVER suddenly jumps in front of the boy and
stands between him and the men)*

SILVER.   Avast there, Tom Morgan.   Maybe you
think you're cap'n here.   By the powers I'll teach
you better.   Have I lived this many years and a son
of a rum puncheon cock his hat athwart my hawse
at the latter end of it?   Well, I'm ready.   Take a
cutlass—him that dares—and I'll see the color of
his insides.   *(As the men all draw away in a group
and whisper together)*   I'm cap'n here by 'lection
and because I'm the best man by a long sea mile.
You won't fight; then by thunder you'll obey—I
like that boy—he's more man than any pair of rats
of you here and—let me see him that'll lay a hand
on him.   *(During this part of the speech the men
have come back with MERRY at their head)*   Well,
you seem to have something to say.   Pipe up and
let me hear it.

MERRY.   Ax your pardon, sir, you're pretty free
with some of the rules; maybe you'll kindly keep
your eye on the rest——

SILVER.   Meanin' by that?

MERRY.   This crew's dissatisfied.   This crew don't
vally bullying a marlin spike.   This crew has rights
—and by your own rules we can talk together—I ax
your pardon, sir, acknowledging you as capting at
this present, but I claim my right and step inside for
a council.   *(With an elaborate sea-salute he marches
into the log house—" One after another the rest
followed his example, each making a salute as he
passed.")*

ARROW. Crew's right. (*Salutes and goes in*)

DICK. According to rules. (*Salutes and goes in*)

MORGAN. Fo'c's'le council. (*Salutes and goes in*)

DIRK. Aye, sir—Fo'c's'le council.

SILVER. (*Intensely and confidentially as soon as they're gone*) Jim, you're within half a plank of death.

JIM. (*Draws back at the idea of torture*) What are they going to do?

SILVER. First they're going to tip me the Black Spot.

JIM. Same as Billy Bones?

SILVER. Aye—(*Takes* JIM *by the arm*) But I'm going to stand by you, lad, through thick and thin.

JIM. (*Surprised*) What!

SILVER. I'll confess I didn't mean to till you spoke up and told about that ship—Once I looked into the bay and seen her gone—well, I'm tough but I gave out—ship gone—neck gone—that's about the size of it. (*Intensely to* JIM) Sure you've got her hidden?

JIM. (*Sits log* R.) I'll not tell where——

SILVER. And I'm not going to ask—but—(*With intensity*) You're sure she's safe?

JIM. Yes—sure——

SILVER. That being the case, why did the doctor give me that? (*Draws out the chart surreptitiously*)

JIM. What?

SILVER. (*As* JIM *looks startled*) Aye, look at it—is that the right one—is it?

JIM. (*Impassioned*) I don't know how you got this—what torture you put them to—to make them give it to you—but you'll never get that treasure—never.

SILVER. Eh?

JIM. I've got that ship, and I've got her hidden, and I am not going to tell you where she is—no matter what you do—never—never—You may get the treasure but we've got the ship, Mr. Silver, and we won't give her up.

SILVER. Aye, lad—a proper spirit, but just now I'm thinking I'm your last card here and by the living thunder, you're mine—I'll save your life so be I can—from them in there—but tit for tat—you save Long John when the time comes.

JIM. I'll do what I can.

SILVER. A bargain. Now, understand—I'm on the Squire's side and I know you've got that ship hidden. (*As* JIM *starts to protest*) There, lad, I'm not asking but I know when a game's up—I do and I know a lad that's staunch—ah, you that's young—you and me might have done a power of good together.

JIM. (*As the men re-appear on the porch*) Here they come!

SILVER. Stand up plucky—and by thunder I still have a shot in my locker. (*As the buccaneers hesitate to approach*) Well, step up. I won't eat you. Which has it? You? Merry——

MERRY. (*Comes timidly forward*) Aye, sir.

SILVER. Well, hand it over, lubber—I know the rules—I won't hurt a deputation. (MERRY *hands* SILVER *a piece of paper.* SILVER *glances at it and then hands it to* JIM) Jim, do you know what that is?

JIM. The Black Spot.

SILVER. Right you was. (*Looks over* JIM'S *shoulder*) Hello. Look here, now—where would you say that was cut from?

JIM. The Bible, sir—see it reads! "Without are dogs and murderers."

SILVER. And very fitting, too. What fool's cut a Bible—you—Merry——

MERRY. Aye—aye, sir?

SILVER. Well, no good'll come of it—you'll swing for it—it ain't lucky.

MERRY. Aye, aye, sir. Oh, ain't it. This crew has tipped you the Black Spot in full council, as in dooty bound—just you turn it over and see what's wrote there——

SILVER. Thanky, George—you always was brisk for business. Well, what is it? (*Turns it over and reads*)   D-e-p-p-o-s-e-d—Dep-posed—and   very pretty wrote, I swear.

MERRY. Come, you don't fool this crew no more, you're over now.

SILVER. Thought you said you knowed the rules?

MERRY. Well?

SILVER. Well, according to rules—I'm still your cap'n till you outs with your grievances and I reply.

MERRY. Alright, then. First and last you made a hash of this cruise. And now for some reason, you're holding back that boy from us—You've bungled the whole thing.

SILVER. Bungled is it? You say—bungled?

MORGAN. (*And the men*) Aye—aye—bungled.

SILVER. Aye, by gum, if you could see how bad it's bungled. We're that near the gibbet my neck's stiff with thinking on it. And do you know all that stands between us and to swing and sun-dry? That boy. He may be our last chance—by thunder you've neither senses nor memory—I let the Squire and his friends go. Alright. And do you want to know why? Well, that's why? (*Takes out the map and throws it on the ground*) I got what I wanted—I got the map. (*As the men pick up the map and look at it*) Aye, look at it—mull it over, you rum puncheons—is it the real one this time or not?

MORGAN. J. F. and a score below.

MERRY. With a close hitch in it.

ARROW. Flint's fist—blood and bones, mate. It's the map, we've got the map.

ALL. Long John—Long John Silver——

SILVER. So that's your true word.

ALL. Captain Silver—Captain Silver, Captain forever.

MORGAN. Come mates, picks and shovels.

DICK. Aye, the treasure—Flint's treasure chest—

MERRY. (*As they get things*) Wait!

MORGAN. Well?

MERRY. When we do find this money how are we to get it home and us no ship.

MORGAN. By the powers, that's right!

ARROW. (*Appealing to* SILVER) Long John——

MERRY. Aye—then tell us that—Silver, tell us that——

ALL. Aye—how—how——

SILVER. By the powers, but you ain't got the invention of a cockroach—You can't find a way to get that money home—not you—It's Silver—Silver—Well then, I tell you—there's your map and that's the way to Flint's treasure—chest—picks—and shovels it is—and once we find it—then by thunder if this lad doesn't lead us to that boat I'll cut his heart out.

OMNES. That's right—Kill him——

JIM. Long John——

CURTAIN.

ACT IV.

SCENE 2:—*The Spy-glass Mountain—a heavily wooded mountain side, with trees and shrubs on all sides, and a thick undergrowth terminating in a large tree at center and up, the base of which alone can be seen. In front of this tree there is a small plateau, grown up on every side with shrubs. At right among the shrubs and partly concealed by them a skeleton, with hands*

*over its head pointing to tree and feet extended
in opposite direction.*

*When the curtain rises, the pirates with the
exception of* DICK *are seen grouped around*
SILVER *and studying the map.* DICK *sits upon
a log, a little apart, his head in his hands as if
sick.*

MORGAN.   Read it out, Barbacue!

SILVER.   (*Reads from map*)   Tall tree—Spy-
glass shoulder, bearing a point to the N. of N. N. E.
Skeleton Island E. S. E. and by E. ten feet.

MERRY.   This is Spy-glass shoulder——

MORGAN.   And plenty of big trees——

MERRY.   Enough for all of us and more——

ARROW.   He buried it well—Flint did—in a
wicked spot.

DICK.   (*Starts up*)   Listen——

SILVER.   What?

DICK.   (*Frightened*)   That's the third time——

MORGAN.   Eh?   Third time of what?

DICK.   It sounds like someone crying——

SILVER.   It's a touch of the sun you've got, Dad—
(*Turns to study his map*)

DICK.   I tell you I heard it—heard it clear——

SILVER.   (*Reading from the map*)   Tall-tree—
Spy-glass shoulder bearing a point to the N. of N. N.
E.   (*Turns to the men*)   Well, lads here we are—
scatter and look—try every tree—keep an eye for
some sign—Scatter with you—(*The men spread
about the mountain, looking at different trees.   To*
JIM *who has seated himself*)   Come, lad.

JIM.   I'm tired sir——

SILVER.   Come.   (*Low to* JIM)   It's no time
to be tired lad—we're getting near the treasure chest.
Keep a sharp watch for whatever happens——

DICK.   (*Suddnly cries out*)   There—there—it is
again!   (*Comes running up to* SILVER)   Don't you

hear it? Don't you? (*As* SILVER *stares at him*)
It isn't the sun—I did hear it, I tell you——
SILVER. (*With meaning to* JIM) Jim, you hear
anything?
JIM. No, sir——
DICK. None the less I did hear it—I know I
did—(*As* SILVER *turns away. Suddenly* MORGAN,
upon the hillside, gives a shout) There—you see—
SILVER. What is it, Tom? (*He and all the men
rush to where stands* MORGAN *who is regarding a
skeleton he has found*) What is it?
MORGAN. Look there—(*The men all look and
then draw back*)
MERRY. By the powers—a skeleton.
DICK. I know I heard something!
ARROW. Now, who d'ye think that might be?
MORGAN. (*Bends over*) He was a seaman—
leastways this is good sea-cloth.
MERRY. You wouldn't think to find a bishop
here, I reckon.
SILVER. (*Who has been studying the skeleton*)
Aye—but what sort of a way is that for bones to
lie?
MORGAN.   Hands   pointing   one   way—feet
t'other——
MERRY. Like a blessed diver he is——
SILVER. Tain't in natur'——
MORGAN. It ain't, and that' a fact.
SILVER. Lads, I'm thinkin' if this could be one
of Flint's jokes now? (*As the men question*) Six
came ashore when he buried the treasure—none
came back. Could this fellow be one of 'em now.
(*Examines the skeleton*) Long bones—and hair's
been yellow——
DIRK. Allerdyes!
SILVER. Aye, that might be Allerdyes—You
mind him, Merry?
MERRY. Aye, that I do—he owed me money, he
did—and took my knife ashore with him——

Morgan. Well, there's little enough about him now—not a thing left—not a copper doit—nor a baccy box——

Merry. That's queer—Flint weren't a man to pick a seaman's pocket.

Silver. By thunder, that's right.

Merry. It don't look nat'ral to me.

Silver. No, by gum, it don't—not nat'ral and not nice—great guns, messmates, but if Flint was living now, this would be a hot spot for you and me. Six they were and six are we: and bones is what they are now.

Dick. (*Starts up*) There! There it is again—

Silver. Avast there, Dick. Flint's dead.

Merry. Aye, I saw him with these here dead-lights—Billy Bones took me in. And there he lay with penny pieces in his eyes.

Dick. Aye, but if ever sperrit walked it would be Flint's——

Merry. Dear heart, but he died hard.

Morgan. Raged and hollered for rum and sang "Fifteen Men."

Merry. It was main hot and the windy was open and I hear that old song comin' out as clear as clear—and the death-haul on the man already.

Silver. Come stow that talk—Flint's dead and he won't walk.

Dirk. He's wise who could say that——

Silver. And as for this fellow here. (*Points to skeleton*) I've taken a notion in my old numbskull, Flint hauled him here and laid him down by compass.

Morgan. What for?

Silver. For a p'inter.

Merry. What! (*There is general excitement among the men*)

Silver. (*To* Morgan *to whom he hands compass*) Tom, here's a compass—just take a bearing along the line of them bones. I'm thinking maybe

there's the signs we're looking for, mates. Well?
MORGAN. (*While the men wait eagerly*) E. S.
E. and by E.
SILVER. (*Reads from map*) And the chart
reads—E. S. E. and by E. It was one of Flint's
jokes and no mistake. There's our way, lads, to
Flint's treasure. Up with you men—up with you—

(*The men with cries start up.*)

DICK. (*Suddenly*) Wait! Wait! (*The men
turn angrily*) You must hear it now—you must—

(*From the distance and in a weird voice there is
heard.*)

" Fifteen men on a dead man's chest.
Yo—ho—ho—and a bottle of rum, etc.

(*There is sudden consternation among the pirates
as they stop stunned.*)

MERRY. (*In awed whisper*) Flint's voice.
MORGAN. Aye, and his song!
DICK. I told you I heard it—I told you.
MERRY. He were an ugly debil, were Flint—and
that blue in the face——
MORGAN. Blue—that's the word.
ARROW. That was how the rum took him.
SILVER. (*Suddenly recovering*) Come—come—
this won't do. Stand by to go about!
MERRY. No—no, Long John.
SILVER. This is only someone sky-larking—
someone that's flesh and blood.
MORGAN. It was Flint's way of singing——
MERRY. Aye, and his tones—I'll swear to that.
SILVER. I tell you it's flesh and blood and I'll
prove it to you—I'm going up there—those of you
who are not white-livered rats will come after me.

(*He starts up the mountain and the others begin timidly to follow*)

DICK. Stop! Oh, stop!

SILVER. Now, by the powers, Dick, another word and I'll run you through.

DICK. Listen.

(*In terror they all stop and there comes from the distance a wailing voice.*)

VOICE. Darby M'Graw—Darby M'Graw—Darby M'Graw.

MERRY. (*In terrified whisper*) Listen to that.

MORGAN. (*The same*) Aye.

VOICE. Fetch aft the rum, Darby M'Graw.

MERRY. That fixes it. They was his last words.

MORGAN. No one on this island ever heard of Darby but us here.

MERRY. It's Flint, mates—I'm going back. Belay there.

SILVER. I never feared Flint alive and by the powers I'll face him dead.

MERRY. Belay there, John—don't you cross the sperrit.

SILVER. Sperrit—well, maybe—why, you rum puncheon if you had listened you'd ha'e noticed an echo.

MERRY. Well?

SILVER. Well, no man has ever seen a sperrit with a shadow. Well, then, what's he doin' with an echo to him, eh? And as for that voice it may be like Flint's but it's a deal more like another's.

MORGAN. Whose?

SILVER. Ben Gunn's.

MERRY. By the powers, it is.

JIM. (*Startled*) Ben Gunn?

SILVER. Aye, Ben Gunn. That's who it is.

DICK. But Ben Gunn ain't alive any more'n Flint.

MERRY. Sho! Nobody minds Ben Gunn—dead or alive.

DICK. Let's turn back, Silver.

MORGAN. Aye—back it is——

SILVER. No, by thunder, no—I'm here to get that stuff and I'll not be beat of man or devil— There's 700,000 pounds up there—and when did ever a gentleman of fortune show his stern to that much, and for a boosy old seaman and him dead. So, up with you—here's our line for the Pole star and the jolly dollars. (*By this time he has reached the plateau. The minute he sees it he draws back*) Come on with you——

(*With a shout the men all go up and shout through following.*)

ARROW. Come on, mate.

MERRY. Up, lads, up——

DICK. All together, now——

(MORGAN *who has gone on ahead gives shout and the men rush to him.*)

SILVER. What——

MORGAN. It's here—Flint's treasure chest——

(*Shouts—all dig.*)

SILVER. (*With* JIM *advances*)   the living rovers, that's right. In with you and dig—dig away——

MORGAN. Not a thing—not a—coin——

SILVER. And do you think you'd find it on the top—no—dig, I tell you, dig.

MORGAN. A two guinea piece.

SILVER. Ah—what did I say—Flint buried it deep—you'll find it——

ARROW. A board with Walrus written on it——

SILVER. Flint's ship—you're getting close to it now—700,000 pounds—think of that—lads—Fortunes for all of us, 700,000 pounds—all of Flint's treasure—all of—(*Stops and thunders loudly*) by all the powers——

JIM. What?

SILVER. Gone——

MORGAN. Aye, gone—not a blessed thing more—

DICK. Fooled.

MORGAN. Beaten.

DICK. Tricked.

MERRY. Aye, lads, tricked; and it's that old cripple there as has done it—that's why he's protected that boy——

SILVER. Stand by for trouble, lad. It's you and me agin the five.

MERRY. Look at the face of him and you'll see it written there—He's sold us, mates—sold us——

OMNES. Kill 'im—kill 'im—(*Gather forward*)

SILVER. Stop—the first one that puts a foot across that rim I fire.

MERRY. Then, by thunder—ye'll have to fire—here goes——

(*Shooting of* MERRY *and other pirate.*)

ARROW. My lads, we've got 'em.

(SILVER *draws cutlass. Pirates start—shots off-stage—fall.*)

SILVER. (*As they start to approach, draws cutlass*) Stand back or by the powers——

MORGAN. We've got you, Long John. We're three to one; now then, mates, from all sides,—all together—Now——

(*Charge and shots are heard—*GUNN, GRAY *and* DOCTOR *rush in.*)

Dr. Livesey. Jim!

Silver. Safe, sir. I've got the lad safe—Ben Gunn!

Gunn. Aye, I'm Ben Gunn, I am—How do, Mr. Silver—Pretty well, thank you, says you——

Silver. And to think it's you whose done me—Ben Gunn, by gum!

CURTAIN.

ACT IV.

Scene 3:—Ben Gunn's Cave.

Jim. (*Discovered and* Ben Gunn *packing gold in bags*) English and French, Spanish and Portuguese Louis—and Georges, doubloons and double guineas, moidores and sequins—look—pictures of all the kings and those strange Oriental pieces with wisps of string like spiders webs.

Ben Gunn. Aye, lad, there it is-—Flint's treasure, all of it. Three years, day by day—it took Ben Gunn to fetch it here.

Jim. What a fortune to be taking home.

Ben Gunn. Home—aye, that's it, lad. Home—you'll be taking me with you, lad, you'll not be leaving Ben Gunn.

Jim. The Squire has given his word.

Ben Gunn. Aye, that he has. That night you came here for my boat—and sent me to him—" Squire," says I. " Jim Hawkins has sent me and tells me as how you are all in a clover hitch. Well, says I, let's bargain—Flint's treasure for a passage home—" " Done," says he.

Jim. And you can rely on that, Ben Gunn.

Squire. (*Without*) Ahoy, shipmates, ahoy.

Jim. What's that?

BEN GUNN. (*Rushes to entrance of cave*) They're here, mates—and look—the ship—she's at anchor. They got her safe——

(GUNN *stays outside watching ship until curtain. Enter* SMOLLETT, SQUIRE, DR. LIVESEY, GRAY, JOYCE *and* SILVER.)

SQUIRE. Jim, my lad, we found the Hispaniola just where you left her—there she rides and now, lads, it's home—home and fortune for us all.

SILVER. (*Slips up*) Aye, aye, sir.

SQUIRE. John Silver, you are a prodigious villain and monstrous impostor.

SILVER. Yes, sir.

SQUIRE. But because you stood by this boy I am told not to prosecute you—but dead men, sir, hang about your neck like millstones.

SILVER. Thank you kindly, sir.

SQUIRE. I dare you to thank me—stand back and now men, to load—to load——

DR. LIVESEY. Wait, Jim Hawkins.

JIM. Yes, sir.

DR. LIVESEY. Jim, there is not a man here but recognizes that if we have found this treasure and are taking it safe home—we owe it all to you. I am proud of you, lad—Gentlemen, I propose a salute to Jim Hawkins, officer of the crown.

ALL. (*Saluting*) Jim Hawkins.—(*Ad lib.*)

CURTAIN.

WHITE BUFFALO
Don Zolidis

Drama / 3m, 2f (plus chorus)/ Unit Set
Based on actual events, WHITE BUFFALO tells the story of the miracle birth of a white buffalo calf on a small farm in southern Wisconsin. When Carol Gelling discovers that one of the buffalo on her farm is born white in color, she thinks nothing more of it than a curiosity. Soon, however, she learns that this is the fulfillment of an ancient prophecy believed by the Sioux to bring peace on earth and unity to all mankind. Her little farm is quickly overwhelmed with religious pilgrims, bringing her into contact with a culture and faith that is wholly unfamiliar to her. When a mysterious businessman offers to buy the calf for two million dollars, Carol is thrown into doubt about whether to profit from the religious beliefs of others or to keep true to a spirituality she knows nothing about.

COCKEYED
William Missouri Downs

Comedy / 3m, 1f / Unit Set

Phil, an average nice guy, is madly in love with the beautiful Sophia. The only problem is that she's unaware of his existence. He tries to introduce himself but she looks right through him. When Phil discovers Sophia has a glass eye, he thinks that might be the problem, but soon realizes that she really can't see him. Perhaps he is caught in a philosophical hyperspace or dualistic reality or perhaps beautiful women are just unaware of nice guys. Armed only with a B.A. in philosophy, Phil sets out to prove his existence and win Sophia's heart. This fast moving farce is the winner of the HotCity Theatre's GreenHouse New Play Festival. The St. Louis Post-Dispatch called Cockeyed a clever romantic comedy, Talkin' Broadway called it "hilarious," while Playback Magazine said that it was "fresh and invigorating."

Winner!
of the HotCity Theatre GreenHouse New Play Festival

"Rocking with laughter...hilarious...polished and engaging
work draws heavily on the age-old conventions of farce:
improbable situations, exaggerated characters, amazing
coincidences, absurd misunderstandings, people hiding
in closets and barely missing each other as they run in and
out of doors...full of comic momentum as Cockeyed hurtles
toward its conclusion."
- Talkin' Broadway

BLUE YONDER
Kate Aspengren

Dramatic Comedy / Monolgues and scenes
12f (can be performed with as few as 4 with doubling) / Unit Set

A familiar adage states, "Men may work from sun to sun, but women's work is never done." In Blue Yonder, the audience meets twelve mesmerizing and eccentric women including a flight instructor, a firefighter, a stuntwoman, a woman who donates body parts, an employment counselor, a professional softball player, a surgical nurse professional baseball player, and a daredevil who plays with dynamite among others. Through the monologues, each woman examines her life's work and explores the career that she has found. Or that has found her.